Night on the
Haunted Highway

MARK W. LESLIE

MARK W LESLIE

NIGHT ON THE HAUNTED HIGHWAY

<u>Prelude</u>
9 pm Highway 166 Texas

Connie Kane is driving her, and her young kids to meet her husband, their father in Houston, but as many of the residents in the area warned her, route 166 is not where you want to be at night at this hour. "Dammit, dammit!" she thinks out loud "I should've listened to the Sheriff, and that crazy man. We, I should've just got a room and stayed the night." "I been driving for hours, we're almost out of gas, and there seems to be no one or nothing in sight." Her son wakes up "Uh, Mommy. Who are you talking to?" she replies "No one baby, I was just thinking out loud." then he asks, "Are you okay mommy?" she answers "Uh, well we're almost out of gas. We'll have to walk until we can find some help." she adds, "It's dark, and scary out there." He sits up and says, "I'm not afraid!" she asks "Why not?" "Cause I'm Cornwallis Kane!" she asks, "Who is?" he says "Son of Cornelius Kane!" she asks, "Who is?" he boast "The toughest S. O. B. in the US Army!" she adds "That's your father!" they laugh.

Without warning the car starts to shake and sputter. It stops dead on the road "Well, that's it Corny. We're out of gas. Wake your sister we got some walking to do. A half-hour later, "Mommy, I'm tired of walking." said little Cassie Kane "I know baby" Connie answered, Cornwallis points ahead as he yells "Look, mommy! What's that red box over there?" She looks and answers "That's an emergency phone box Corny. We can use it to call for help." as they run to it Cornwallis asks "Why would they put a phone on the side of the road?" she answers "Some highways have them in case of an accident, or if someone runs out of gas, like us. Eh like me." Cornwallis replies "Don't say it like that mommy. It's not your fault." she says "Yes, it is Corny. It's all my fault." She opens the box, grabs the phone, and smiles as she starts to dial "We can call for some help, so we'll be Just fine." "BEEP, BEEP, BEEP, I'm sorry, but this unit is no longer in service." the phone sounded "No, no, no, no!" she yells as she slams the phone back into the box, she says "This can't be happening. This just can't be happening!"

Both Cornwallis and Cassie are shocked by their mother's reaction. Cornwallis looks up at her and says "It's okay mommy. Let's just keep walking till we find some to help." Cassie speaks "But I'm so tired, my feet hurt. Carry me mommy." Cornwallis interjects "No Cassie, it's too far for mom to carry you. You're not a baby anyone. You're a big girl now, and too heavy for mom to carry."

Cassie drops her head Cornwallis extends his hand and says "Grab my hand sis, walk with me." she takes his hand, and they start walking, he looks down at his sister asking "You're not scared are you?" she looks up at her big brother smiles, and answers "Not while you're here Corny." He smiles at her as they continue walking. Connie thinks to herself *"I really made a mess of things, but I'm so proud of my Corny. He's so much like his father."* she smiles.

NIGHT ON THE HAUNTED HIGHWAY

__Elsewhere in the small town of Goodwind__
__Texas, at the home of Frankie Lee__

The local sheriff is banging on the front door, yelling "Frankie! Frankie Lee! Open the Dam Door! "You hear me?! Frankie?! You son of a B..." Just then the door opens, Frankie stands there smiling as he speaks "Sheriff Buckley, come on in friend. Welcome." as Buckley walks in closing the door behind him Frankie asks "What brings you here my old friend?" Buckley's nostrils flared, he answers, "You know why the hell I'm here!" He continues "Why Frankie? Why did you tell that woman with the two kids, what was gonna happen to them on the highway? You know what happens when anyone tells outsiders the full details of driving on 166 at night..." Frankie cuts him off "Yeah, yeah, I know Buck. You'll be dead by the next morning. Whatever evil thing is out there, it doesn't seem to like it when you try to warn people about it." Buckley says "Dammit Frankie. Why? You saw what happened to Jessie May Years ago." Frankie answers "Because I'm tired Buck. I'm sick of watching people riding to their death down that road to hell, and all we can do give subtle little hints of trouble. We come off sounding like crazy old-town folk from a horror film! No wonder most of them don't want to listen to us." Buck says "You know that some people are gonna do whatever the hell they want to. We couldn't talk them out of driving even if we showed them pictures of what would happen. So they end up dead cause they're hardheaded, and one of us ends up dead because we told too much."

Frankie responds, "Yeah Buck I know, here take this." "A key?" Buckley asked, "What's the key for?" an eerie moment of silence took over the conversation as they both looked towards a large foot locker. Frankie speaks "In the morning you will find all my affairs in order Buck." Buckley shakes his head saying, "You bastard, you've planned this whole thing?!"

Buck's eyes start to get a little misty, he turns his back to Frankie. Frankie places his hand on Buckley's shoulder and says, "It's very important to me, old friend that you let everyone in town know just how much I love them, how much I love being a part of this ll community. Everyone here is family to me. Can you tell everyone that, Buck?" Buckley responds "Uh, yeah Frank, we uh love you too buddy. This place won't be the same without you man."

Frankie smiles and says, "Who knows, this thing, whatever it is, might just skip me tonight. I might be alive in the morning." still turned away from Frankie, Buckley replies "Well, if that's the case, let's go fishing in the morning." "I'll like that, Buck." "Yeah, me too Frankie." "See you around Buck." "Yeah Frankie, see you in the morning."

Buckley leaves, not once looking back at Frankie. Once outside after Frankie closed the door Buckley looks back at the house and says to himself "Dammit Frankie, dammit. I'm gonna miss you." he heads to his car. Inside Frankie is sitting on his bed looking at the many photos of him, Buckley, and all his other friends of Goodwind. He placed the strap book on the nightstand, he lays down with his arms crossed, he takes a deep breath, he closes his eyes.

Back on the highway 166

Connie and the kids are still walking when they finally see a house off the street. She says "Look guys, maybe we can find some help there." as she points toward the house, Cassie says "Mommy it looks scary." Cornwallis responds "Well, I'm not afraid, Let's go." They head towards it.

At the front door, Connie rings the bell, and knocks a few times Yelling "Hello! Hello! Is anyone there? We're lost, and out of gas. Can you help us? Hello?!" The door opens, they hear an old voice *"Come in, come in sweat ones."* As they walk in Cornwallis notices "Mommy there's no one here. But I heard a voice." She answers "I know baby, I heard it too." Cassie cries "Mommy, mommy I'm scared. Let's go back outside." Just then the door slams "BAM!" Connie says, "The door, it's locking itself!" Cassie cries "What happening, mommy?!" Connie grabs Cassie and says, "I don't know baby, I don't know!" An eerie voice calls out. *"Do not worry Sweet Ones. We are going to take good care of you."* Cornwallis yells "Where is that voice coming from?!"

Cassie yells "Augh! mommy what is that!" she reacts "I don't know, it's horrible!" they both start to scream as it rushes towards them, Cornwallis jumps in front of his family and yells "Stay behind me I'll protect you!" Connie grabs him and pulls him behind her with Cassie, the two children hug each other as they close their eyes, Connie yells as she holds onto her babies "Stay back! go, go away, don't you harm my... Her last words spoken, all that is heard are their screams as a monstrous voice speaks,

"Ah, Sweet Ones!"

<u>Chapter 1</u>
Ready for Spring Break

In America many believe that they can say and do whatever they want, go wherever they like, and do as they please. Stepping into areas where no one should never be caught standing in. To those who feel so entitled, so headstrong that no one, or no rule can tell them anything. But life has a way of saying, Not so fast.

<u>*University College*</u>

The Highland Kings of Oklahoma, just north of the Texas border known for it's athletic program which is second to none. Not for winning championships (which are few, and far in between), but they're known as an all-athletic school (academics be dammed). Every student here is an athlete playing one of the many sports that the school has to offer. No other school in the world has as many sports teams. From A to Z if it's a known sport, you better believe that the **Highland Kings of University College** has a team competing in somebody's conference, league, or division.

<u>*Friday 9 am Cafeteria*</u>

Bernard "Biff" Becker and Donald "Dale" Dole just finished eating, and are heading toward the door. Biff says "Hey, Dale." Dale answered "What's up?" Biff asks "How's things with you, and Tiff?" Dale answers "We're good man. Why you ask?" Biff responds "You haven't done it yet, have you?" Dale says "Hey man handle your own business, stay out of mine." Biff says "Oh, I'm gonna handle my business, when we get to Gunther Beach this weekend." he continues "But now it's time to handle your business Dale." Dale answers "Yeah whatever." Biff grabs Dale's shoulders and turns him toward one of their classmates, saying "Look dude over there, who do you see?" Dale answers "That's Stacy Sullivan, right? She's on the women's bodybuilding team." Biff replies "Yeah and for a bodybuilder, she's a knockout." "And you should see her without any clothes on." Dale responds "Yeah, I know you told me, you guys had a lot of fun that night. What does that have to do with me." Biff explains "Dude why do you think she keeps looking over here smiling. "Those smiles are't for me man. They're for you." Dale answers "What? No, get out of here with that." Biff explains "Listen, dude. She has agreed to help you with your little problem." puzzled Dale asks, "Problem? What prob....?" Biff interrupts yelling out "She, said she would love to bust your cherry dude! She said tonight if you're ready, or whenever!" Stacy smiles as others heard Biff's words laughs, she blows Dale a kiss. Embarrassed Dale waves, and gives her a fake smile, turns to Biff "I can't believe you did that. Not cool dude." Dale storms off. Biff yells "Hey Stacy, we'll get back to you, but keep the motor running, he's a little scared! You know first time and all!" he blows her a kiss as he runs off to catch up with Dale.

Biff catches up with Dale, angrily Dale yells "Hey man never do that again!" Biff says "Alright, alright sorry dude. I was just having fun and thought I could help a virgin out." Dale says "Well thanks a lot, don't do me any more favors. I'm saving myself for Tiff, okay." Biff responds "Yeah Tiffany the Tease. You might as well be a monk waiting on Tiffany opens up those skinny legs." Dale says "Yeah right, and what about you, and your big plans this weekend?" Biff asks "What about it?" Dale answers "Well you've been talking about you, hitting all the booty on the beach you can, but not while Beck is on your arm. You're not gonna get to have any fun at all." Biff responds "Hey Becky and I always have fun and lots of it. Becky and I are going to enjoy our Spring Break. Hey by the way. Where are the others." As they head outside, Dale thinks to himself *"Well Stacy is sexy though."*

Meanwhile outside in the Main Courtyard

Bethany "Becky" Bradshaw, Tyler "Tiffany" Thomas, and Deanna "Donna" Dean are walking towards the cafeteria building. Becky says "Hey we need to get a move on before the guys take off. I just hope the cafeteria serves something good for a change." Donna says, "Dream on girl." they all laugh, Tiffany says, I can't wait till we get to Gunther Beach." Donna says "You got that right. I got a special outfit just for the trip." Becky asks "Hey Tiff, how did you talk boring Dale into going on the trip anyway?" Tiffany responds "Dale not boring." Donna says "Beck she did the same thing to Dale that you did to Biff. She work that booty all in his face till he gave in." Tiffany smile saying, "No I didn't." Becky says, "I did."

Out of nowhere Raymond Ray-Ray Pierce joins the party "Hello ladies." "And especially you babe." as he and Donna embrace in a passionate kiss. Becky thinks to herself *"I wish Biff would kiss me like that."* Ray-Ray says "Ladies I must warn you. Today's special at the greasy spoon is their famous Mystery meat with green eggs." Both Becky and Tiffany says, "For breakfast Gross!" Donna says to Ray "Hey, baby I can't wait till our trip. And I got a surprise for you." Ray answers, "Oh yeah?" Donna replies "Oh yeah." Ray looks down the way and says "Oh no. Looks like Pookie found him some trouble." Donna says "Humph, or trouble found him. Ray do we have to bring him along too?" Becky says "Yeah Ray seven a crowd." Ray answers "Ladies I know, but if I was to leave him here by himself our beloved school would be burned to the ground. And that if he was being good." the girls laugh, Ray says to Donna "Catch you later babe." Donna replies "Okay baby." They kiss. "Later ladies, oh, and tell the guys I'll catch them later at practice." He turns toward Pookie's direction "Hey, Yo, Pookie, wait up!" he starts to run after him.

Becky says "You're so lucky Donna, I wish Biff would kiss me the same way Ray kisses you." Donna responds "He will just give him some time." Tiffany says "Guys let's go eat I'm hungry." Moments later as Ray catches up with Percival "Pookie" Prior he asks him "Pookie!, What the hell you're doing man?" Pookie answers "Man they disrespected me, and I'm...", "Gonna what Pook?" Ray interrupts "You gonna take on five guys at once?" Smart Pook real smart." Pookie says "Well, what I'm supposed to do?" Ray answers "What you're supposed to do. Pook. why are you here?" Pookie answers "What?" "You heard me Pook. Why are you here?" Pookie answers mockingly, "To get an education, so I can be all I can be." Ray says "That's right and lately you been acting like and straight fool, if you didn't have the highest grade-point average in the school's history, they would've kicked you out once you quit the football team." Pookie says "Well? Ray answers Well? Come on Pook, don't make me call Aunt Flo." Pookie answers "Alright, alright. I'll do it your way, just don't call me moms Okay." Ray says "Good cuz good. Let's get to class. And stop talking like a hood rat thug. Boy you're from Long Island." Pookie responds "Man F you, I go hard." they laugh as they head for class.

Later at Track and Cross-Country practice

Tiffany is watching Dale run wind sprints as she's finishing up the last of her warm-ups before her three-mile run. He finally looks toward her, he trots her way, as Tiffany smiles, and drops her head blushing. "Hey Tiff." She answers "What's up baby?" he replies, "Well first off, how about a kiss?" as he leans into her reaching for some sugar, she gently pushes him back as she says, "Come on Dale we're at practice." he quickly answers "So who's gonna care? Everyone knows we're dating." Tiffany says "You know I don't like doing that at practice." "I know, but can you blame a guy for trying?" she smiles as she blushes. Dale says "Anyway, your coach and my coach agreed that I should teach you how to sprint as we do in the 100, and 200 meters, so you will have a stronger finishing kick at the end of your races." "Sprint!" Tiffany yells, no I'm a long-distance running a. k. a. cross country." Dale replies "That's clear babe, but if you learn to finish with a sprinter's kick the last 100, or 200 meters you can better your chances of winning and better your time as well." Tiffany pauses as she thinks it over and says "Well if you and my coach agree on the subject, I guess I can give it a try." she asks, "What do I do first?" Dale answers "Well first you could give your bf a kiss." she smiles saying "Fine." as she kisses him on his cheek, Dale says "Wow, my mom gives me better kisses than that." Tiffany says, "Can we get on with this please." "Okay, okay." Dale says laughing, he says as he shows her "First let's start with the take-off. Down on all fours, place your hand out in front like this. Place your strong leg back, and the other forward." As she sets herself in the position she asks, "Okay now what?" He answers "Now straighten your back out, and your head up." she says "Okay." He adds "Now look down the track and pick a target." "A target?" she asked, "Yeah a target." He answers, "Find a target, fix your eyes on it, and with all you got run to it." She says "Alright, I got one." He tells her "First use your back leg to push off, stay low on your take-off, kick hard only run on your toes. The rest of your foot never touches the ground." He pauses then asks, "You got it?" She answers "It's a lot but, I think so." He replies "Okay let's do this. Down to the end of the track." she says, "I'm ready."

Dale counts it off "Ready, Set, Go!" They take off down the track Dale is running slower than he normally would just so he can stay with Tiffany. She looks at him smiling. He yells "Don't look at me, eyes on your target." She turns her head and continues. Dale slows to a walk as he watches Tiffany finish to the end of the run. She reaches the end stops and tries to catch her breath. Dale walks up to her as she says with excitement "Did you see? Did you see it? I think that's the fastest I ever ran!" Dale leaned to her and says, "That was good babe, but never turn your head, always keep your eyes on your target. And never, ever slow down until you pass your target." She smiles and says "Okay coach." she kisses him on his cheek, and she runs off yelling back at him "See ya at the meeting babe!" He pauses, then yells as he chases after her "Hey Tiff, wait!"

Football Practice in the Weight room

Biff is on the beach as Ray is spotting him. Mark Maryland and the others are cheering him on. "Biff! Biff! Biff! Biff!" they chant, Ray yells out "Come on, come on!, Push it, push you, girly boy! Push, push!" Biff yells out "Augh!" as he pushes the weights up as far as he can. Ray yells "You got it!" as he grabs the bar and helps Biff place it back on the rack, their teammates Jump up in down, yelling as if they won a championship.

Everyone calms down, as Mark speaks "Now, that was intense, but not bad for a tight end with no hands." "No hands uh." Biff says, he continues "I'll remember that the next time you throw one of those ducks, you call a pass on third and long." Ray jumps in and says "Still Biff, you should be a lot stronger than that, for the position that you play." "Position!, Position!" yells Biff, he continues "Look at this body dude. This is not a football body. This is an Olympic-level bodybuilder you're looking at. That's right Apollo, Adonis eat your hearts out. The camera wants this, the judges want this, and Oh yeah, the ladies want this here."

Mark throws a towel at Biff, jokingly saying "Man you ain't shit." Ray adds "Yeah, man if that's your dream, why you're playing football, and not on the bodybuilding team?" Biff answers "Because the coach doesn't want his bodybuilders playing other sports and my dad won't let me quit the football team." Ray asks "Why not?" Mark adds "Yeah, I mean, it's not like we need you anyway." all the guys laugh, and Biff responds "F you, weak arm quarterback. My dad and coach Wayne think I got a real shot at making the League." Ray laughs as he says "Yeah the Canadian League hahaha."

Biff returns the joke "F you dude. I'll see you in the Grey Cup, you eight-round draft pick of a wide receiver." Ray answers "F you son. I have you know I'm one of the fastest wideouts in the nation. That sounds like a first-round pick to me. I'll see you in the Super Bowl." Mark jumps in saying "Yeah says the wideout with no hands, that can't run a route to save his life." Ray answers "I have you know jello arm, that I'm the all-time leading receiver in catches, yards, and touchdowns in this school's history." Mark answers back "That's because the school has been running the wishbone and only threw the ball twice a game. That was before I got here with this cannon of an arm."

Biff flexes as he speaks "Guys, guys, I know this body brings out the worst in others, ladies want it, guys want to be like it, but instead of fighting. All you have to do is work hard and you too can have one like this. Well, not as good, but close." The guys all throw towels and other small objects at Biff as they comment "Ahhh man you just so full of yourself." Biff kisses his biceps and says "I know, I Know."

Cheerleaders' Locker Room just after practice.

The girls are getting dressed, and ready to go back to the classrooms. Donna says to Becky "Hey girl don't forget we got a meeting so we can plan our trip for the break." Becky answers "I won't D." Donna says "I can't wait til we get there."

Just then Linda Lawson yells at them "I bet Gang Bang Becky can't wait either." Missy Monday join in saying to Becky "Yeah ain't that right Gang Bang?" Donna turns her head towards them saying "You two sluts mind your business." Linda replies "Sluts? We're not the sluts around here." Missy says to Becky "Yeah ain't that right Gang Bang." she continues asking Becky "How many guys you're gonna do this weekend?"

Becky drops her head, but Donna can see a tear fall from her face. Donna stands up and walks towards Missy and she too has stood up.

Donna says "I've told you before to leave her alone." Linda stands up and says to Donna "Why don't you let her fight her own battles?" Missy smiles and adds "Yeah, let the whore fight for herself." Donna grabs Missy and pushes her back against the lockers "BAM!",

Donna stares into her eyes saying "Leave her alone!" Linda steps back and says "Are you crazy?!" Missy Yells "Get your hands off me you black bitch." Donna with all she has throws a punch toward Missy "POP!" After a short pause, Missy opens her eyes as she realized that the punch landed on the locker door, she sees the dent left on it and yells "You are crazy!"

Donna smiles saying "Next time bitch the dent will be in your face." Becky jumps up and runs out of the room, Donna calls out "Beck wait!" Linda gently grabs Donna's hand and removes it from Missy's neck, and says "Why don't you just ask your friend what she did to us?" Missy adds "Yeah new girl, ask her."

Donna backs up and heads to catch up with Becky. Donna finds Becky in the hallway crying Donna asks "Beck. What is it with you and them?" Becky wipes her face and asks "What did they tell you?" Donna answers "They told me to ask you."

Becky clams down as she explains "Well just before you got here, I uh, well, I had a threesome with their boyfriends." Shocked Donna says "I see why they hate you. Why? Beck, why did you do that?" Becky answers "I don't know. We were on a class trip, it was the weekend, we had been drinking, and it just happened." Donna asks "How did Linda, and Missy find out?" Becky answers "Linda walked in on us and she was devastated." es "Now the whole school knows, everybody hates me, and Biff is the only guy that would even talk to me, and you see how that goes." Donna responds "Well I haven't been here that long, and Tiffany, I'm sure she knows too. We don't care what happened in the past, you been a really good friend, and we both love you girl."

Becky looks at Donna smiles and says "I love you guys too." Donna says "Now come on let's go to class, and let's not talk about this ever again."

Becky asks "Oh by the way. How's your hand? You didn't break it, did you?" "nah." Donna smiles as she replied "I was a boxer at Tech State, I know how to roll my fist to keep from injuring it." Becky asks "You boxed there, but transferred to cheerleader here, why?" Donna smiles saying "Because all the cute guys don't like tough girls with bruises on the face, and beat up knuckles." They laugh.

Later at the School's Library

The three couples are having their meeting, Biff is in the middle of speaking "So it's agreed. Ladies, you'll take my car, and we guys will be riding with my homie Ray. So on the way down we can talk about movies, and sports, and you ladies get to talk about us."

Ms. Garfield The librarian says, "Hush."

Tiffany responds "That's not funny, How can you say that?" Biff answers "Cause that's what you ladies do." Donna says "That is true Tiff. We do talk about the guys a lot."

The librarian says, "Shush!"

"Oh yeah D? What you been saying about me." Ray asked as he starts kissing around Donna's ear while she starts to giggle. *"Biff never kisses me like that."* Becky thought as she stares at the two.

The librarian says, "Be quiet!!"

Dale says "Hey, Hey guys, guys get a room, please there are minors present." Biff says to Dale the only minor here is you and your Blue nuts" Everyone laughs except Tiff as she says "that's not funny!" Dale replies to Biff "Yeah, Yeah yeah, Laugh it up, you Nerf Herder."

The librarian says, "Shut up!!!"

Biff says "Alright, alright, people in about two hours Spring Break begin. We leave early in the morning. Gunther Beach, Here we come! Everyone claps, screams, and celebrates.

The librarian yells, "That's it you kids got the fuck out of here!!!!"

Later at the School's Child Care Center

Ms. Holly has been waiting for Tiffany, who just walked through the door, and saying, "Hello, Ms. Holly how are you?" Ms. Holly answers "I'm fine, and you." Tiffany replies "I'm great." Ms. Holly says "I can always depend on you to be on time. and the kids, just have been asking if you were coming today." "Really? Tiffany asked, Ms. Holly answers "Yes. I don't know how you do it, but they do respond well to you." Tiffany replies smiling "That's awesome, They're a great group of kids, and I love all of them. I wish I had kids of my own." Ms. Holly pats her on the shoulders, saying "Someday you will, but for now you got them until your replacement gets here at 3:00 o'clock. You might want to check with little Amy first, she has been asking about you the most." Tiffany answers "Okay Ms. Holly I'm on it, you take care."

Tiffany turns and sees Amy, heading right for her. Little Amy yells out "Ms. Tiffany!" all the kids stopped what they were doing and surrounded Tiffany yelling, singing, and saying hello to her. As Ms. Holly walks out the door thinking *"She's some sitter, she'll make a great mother someday."*

Meanwhile

Biff and Dale are heading to science class when Dale asks Biff "Dude, you ready for the test today?" Biff answers "Yea I sure ready to copy every answer you write down, hahaha."

Dale says "Ugh, that's not gonna happen, dude." Biff grabs Dale's shoulder lends into him saying "Look D. forget that, we got to get you laid." "What?" Dale replies, Biff says "Well I tried to hook you up with Stacy, but you ran out. So I was thinking maybe you might want some dark meat."

Dale says "Dark, what? What the hell you're talking about Biff?" Biff answers "Don't think I don't notice how you and Mary Maryland been eyeballing each other. You should go on and tap that." Dale responds "Yeah right, and let, your beloved quarterback kick my ass for missing with his twin sister. No thanks." Biff replies "Mark wouldn't do that. He's a sucker for charity cases like you." Dale smirk saying "Enough dude let's get to class before we're late."

Moments later as they reach their classroom they stop and allow Mary and one of her friends to walk through the door first, as Mary passes by she smiles at Dale and says, "Hey Dale, how you're doing?" Dale answers "Uh, great, how are you, Mary?" He thinks to himself *"Mary is so hot!"* Biff lends into Dale and says, "You want to sit down before were late for class. And wipe that smile off your face you look like a preverb." Dale responds "That's not what the word means." "The word you're looking for is a pervert." Biff answers back "Whatever dude, don't be one."

Sometime later while in the middle of taking their test. Biff tosses a note over to Dale. Dale grabs it and reads...

{Hey dude what's the

answers to questions

2, 7, 8, 9, and 12.}

Dale writes a response, tosses it back to Biff. He reads it, then drops his head in disappointment.

{Go to hell dude, I'm

not getting kicked out of

school for cheating, you

had enough time to study!!!}

A few minutes later the bell rings. Spring Break had begun. For all the students it's open season as the classroom clears out at a record pace, with Biff leading the way. As Dale drops off his test paper Mr. Frost says "Mr. Dole. You continue to amaze me sir." Dale replies "Sir?"

"All year your friend Mr. Becker bags you for answers while taking a test and you continue to deny his request. For that I commend you."

"Mr. Frost, uh how do you know that?" "Your friend Mr. Becker always drops your notes right here in my trash basket and I read them all." "Uh sorry Mr. Frost." "Don't be Mr. Dole in fact with your grades, and integrity I'm recommending you for the school's mentor- ship program." "Wow, really sir?" Dale asked "Yes Mr. Dole you're a step closer to becoming a professor in the field of science." "Wow thank you Mr. Frost," Dale said while shaking his hands.

<u>Tiffany's, and Becky's Dorm Room 7pm</u>

Tiffany and Dale are making out. Dale thinks to himself *"Yes, yes, yes. It's finally gonna happen, I'm finally gonna get some. Yes, yes, come on, come on."*

Tiffany pushes back and yells "Stop, stop enough, Dale!" Dale answers "Wait, What?, What's wrong Tiff? Why you stopped?" Tiffany replays "I'm not ready yet Dale. He answers "What are you kidding me?" "No, I'm not kidding you." "I'm not ready to have sex yet, okay." Dale reacts "Wow, right in the middle of my boner. Biff was right. I am lame."

Tiffany reacts "Biff! Biff! You what to have sex with me just to impress Biff!?" "No, no Tiff that's not what I meant." Tiffany replies "What did you mean?" while rubbing his forehead Dale answers "We've been dating almost a year now Tiff. We should be halfway through every position in the book by now."

"What!" Tiffany screamed, "How could you say that to me Dale? "Is that all you think about is sex?" Dale jokingly answers "Well, not all." Tiffany jumps off the bed.

Tiffany yells "You! You!" she thinks *"I'm so mad I don't know what to say."* Dale stands and says "Tiff you're the one who said you wanted kids, right?" "Well yes, of course, I do. More than anything." she replies, "Well there's only one way to make it happen." he says jokingly Tiffany answers "You're an animal."

"Tiff you said that I was the one, remember?" Tiffany answers "I know what said." "I'm just not ready to go all the way." now Dale yells "Go all the way!?" he finishes "What are we 12?!"

With a frown on her face she says "Don't yell at me." "I'm sorry I didn't mean to Yell at you Tiff." he replies, Tiffany says "Good night Dale." she points toward the door "Tiff," he pleads with his puppy eyes face, She stomps her foot and pointed at the door again.

He drops his head as he says "Okay Tiff." She kisses his cheek and again points at the door and says "Good night Dale." "Good night Tiff" As he walks for the door he thinks to himself *"See I am lame."*

<u>Meanwhile in Biff's and Dale's Dorm</u>
<u>Room</u>

The sounds of moans and groans, yes, oh yes, and Yeah girl right there can be heard from there.

Minutes later Biff takes a deep breath and rolls off Becky saying "Dam girl you went all in that time." he turns over away from her. Becky moves up close so she can snuggle from behind Biff, he speaks "What are you doing Beck?" "I just wanted to snuggle a little." he replies "You know I don't snuggle." she answers "I know, I was just hoping we could, you could be, well be like..." he cuts her off and says "Like Ray!"

"Well I'm not like Ray. If he's what you want, go have sex with him." Becky responds "I don't want Ray, I just want a little romance that's all."

He replies "Yeah, yeah romantic like Ray!" she rebuffs "This isn't about him it's about you, Bernard." "Don't! Call me that!" he adds "You know I don't like being called that."

she responds "Sorry, I just want a little..." he interrupts "What? Love, and tenderness. Some passion maybe." he adds "If its romance you want you can get it from Ray, or our local virgin, he should be here soon. You know Tiffany won't open up and give him some tonight, so there you are."

she asks "What is wrong with you? Why Do you treat me like this? Is all I am to you a piece of meat?" without saying a word Biff turns back over away from her again and thinks to himself *"Hell yeah, and some old meat at that."*

Becky yells "You have nothing to say? Noting?" Biff answers "Yeah, don't let the door hit you." tears starts to roll down her face, and she starts to shake.

She screams "Aghh!!" she begins to get dressed.

Moments later as Becky heads for the door she stops and looks back at Biff "Is there anything you want to say to me." she pleaded, Biff answers "Yeah, don't lock the door, virgin ass probably forgot his key again." as more tears flow down her face she replies "Ass hole!"

Becky swings open the door Dale is there about to use his key "Oh hey Beck. Am I interrupting anything?" Becky answers "Why don't you ask your asshole friend if you're interrupting anything." Dale yells "Hey asshole friend! Am I interrupting anything?" Biff yells back "Yeah, my sleep! We got a big day tomorrow, and we're leaving early! So both of you take your asses to bed!"

Overflowing with tears Becky says to Dale "Your friend's a piece of work." as she walks off Dale replies "My friend's a piece of shit."

Dale closed the door he asks Biff "Why do you treat Beck like that dude?" Biff asks "Did Tiff give you some ass tonight?" Dale answers "No, she didn't" Biff chuckle and says "That's what I thought, go to bed virgin."

Dale turns off the light he mumbles "Dickhead."

NIGHT ON THE HAUNTED HIGHWAY

Meanwhile in Ray's Dorm Room

Ray and Donna are having dinner and a movie night. While sitting on the love seat Donna thinks to herself *"Ray seam so far away from me now, I wonder."*

she asks "What's on your mind baby." Ray stairs at her then replies "What?, Uh, oh yea sorry baby girl. I was just thinking about Pook." Donna sighs and replies "Oh him again." Ray answers "Well he is my cousin."

she replies "Yeah your Hood Rat thug cousin, who should've been kicked out of school a long time ago." he responds "He's not a Hood Rat. He's a want-a-be thug, girl, that boy's an honor student, he has the highest GPA in this school's history. They're not gonna kick him out." "Still he shouldn't quit the team."

She asks "If he's so smart, why does he keep doing dumb shit?" Ray snaps back "I know, I know, it drives me crazy." she says "He's not your responsibility Ray."

He answers "Yes, yes he is. If anything happens to him I'll never hear the end of it. Plus he's my cousin. I love the guy." she asks "And what about me?"

Ray stares deeply into her eyes, and says "Well ah, you're a different kind of Love Baby Girl. You're on a whole new level." She giggles a little as he kisses her.

Meanwhile in Pookie's Dorm Room

He's laying on the bed with multiple thoughts running through his head _"I can't believe those bitch ass mothers tried to punk me in front of everybody. E=mc2. Them bitches don't know who the hell they're messing with. Einstein's theory of special relativity expresses the fact that mass and energy. I can't let this stand. That mass and energy are the same physical entity and can be changed into each other. Those bitches got to respect me. The increased relativistic (m) of a body, times (c2) speed of light. Yeah, I got a rep to uphold. Is equal to (E)_

The kinetic energy of that body. So what am I gonna do about it, wait!, I know what to do."

Just then the door is forced open BAM! Pookie jumps up he sees three dudes he thinks _"Wow these guys mean business."_

He asks "Can I help you, gentlemen?" The leader asks "You're the one they call Pookie around here?" Pookie answers "Yes, Yes I'm Pookie." the leader replies "Let's go Big Joe wants to see you, Kid." "Ah who's Big Joe?" Pookie asked, one of the others answers "He's the Boss, and he don't like waiting on no punk kids when they're asked to pay him a visit."

Pookie responds "Well then we mustn't keep the Boss waiting. Just let me cut my television off and we can go."

As Pookie grabbed the remote off the bed he thinks to himself _"I don't believe these guys are gonna let me do this. First I'll turn off the TV, then sneak on my camera there. I don't think they notice it, so I'll hit the record button and..."_

He turns to the gangsters, smiles, and says "Okay gentlemen. Take me to your leader, what's his name again?"

"Big Joe!" the gangster yells

Pookie smiles saying "Let's go." as he thinks _"Got ya bitch."_

The Next Day
Early Sunrise in the Parking Lot

The gangs all ready for their trap, everyone is happy, excited and full of life "But wait!" Biff yells, "Where the hell is Pookie!?" Dale adds "Yeah Ray he's late." Beck also adds "He's always late. What is it this time?"

Donna responds "He's probably knee-deep in trouble again." Ray looks at his watch "Dam. I'll find his ass." Donna asks "Why don't we just go without him?" Ray answers "You know I can't leave him here by himself. The school won't be standing by the time we get back."

Dale replies "That's true there will be carnage." Ray says "you guys go on ahead. Pookie and I will catch up with you later." Donna reacts "Uh uh, I'm not going without you Ray." Ray makes eye contact with her and says "Baby girl, it's alright, you can go we'll catch up in no time."

Donna repeats "I'm not going without you Ray." they smile and begin to kiss. Becky thinks to herself *"Look at that passionate kiss. Why can't I get a kiss like that from Biff?"*

After the kiss, Ray looks at Biff, and Dale s "Guys Donna and I will meet you at the beach after we find Pookie." Biff asks "You sure Bro?" Ray answers "Yeah Bro,"

They say their goodbyes as the guys do their Bro handshakes and the ladies hug each other, as Ray and Donna walk away Biff says to the others "Alright people it's time to hit the road! Mount up!"

They head for Biff's car Dale ask "Hey, who died and made you Chief Cheese around here?" Biff answers "Your mom appointed me last night after we banged." Tiffany reacts "Gross Biff, real gross."

<u>Chapter 2</u>

On the Road

Biff, Becky, Dale, and Tiffany all get into Biff's car when Dale says "Let's do this." Tiffany says "yes." Becky yells "I can't wait."

Dale comments "Let's just hope Biff doesn't play any of that BS he calls music." Biff responds "Hey dude don't talk smack about my sounds."

He turns on the radio, and yells "Now you telling me you guys don't like this!" as he turns up the volume.

Dale yells "Just play something else please!" as he turns the sounds down.

Becky asks "Are you guys gonna fight over the music all the way to the beach?"

"Nobody asked you" Biff answered.

Tiffany yells at him "Meanie."

Dale says "Yeah man don't be talking to the ladies like that"

Becky adds "Why you're acting like that." Biff replies "Hey I'm trying to enjoy myself dude, I gonna let it all hang out. Are you with me man?"

Dale answers "Hell yeah!"

Tiffany remarks "You guys are a couple of loons."

Becky agrees "Yeah girl real basket cases. We may need to change our minds about riding with them."

Biff yells "Calm down everybody. When you're on the road you need good sounds to get you down! Turn on the tunes, and turn up the volume!" He continues "That's the one, I'm sure you all know the words. Just jump in

on your favorite part."

NIGHT ON THE HAUNTED HIGHWAY

Dale is driving now the others are asleep. He sees a sign for a Quick E-Q Mart. He speaks "Hey Biff, Biff, wake up." Biff's eyes open "Wha, what man, what?"

Dale answers "We need some gas there's a quick stop at the next exit."

Biff says "Yeah, okay do that." then Dale Yells "Alight, alright ladies, wake up, wake up. I'm pulling over to the Quick E-Q for some gas, so if you want to freshen up. Now's the time."

Becky's eyes cracked open "Uh what, oh yeah okay." she responds saying "Tiff, Tiff wake up." as she shakes her "We're making a pit stop girl."

Tiffany's eyes open "Yeah, yeah okay I'm up."

Dale yells "You girls were sleeping so good. Sorry, we had to wake you."

Biff interrupts "Yeah but we got some nice pictures of you two."

Becky yells "What!" Tiffany says "You better not have."

Dale answers "Yeah we did."

Biff says "I can't wait to show them all over the school when we get back Hahaha!

Becky Yells "You basters!"

Tiffany "You guys better not show them."

Laughing Dale says "Relax ladies." We're just Joking with you. We got no pictures Ha ha."

Biff adds "Ha, wish we did, you should have seen the look on your faces haha."

Becky swings her pocketbook across the back of Biff's head saying "You rat, don't you play with me like that!" Biff laughs harder.

Tiffany asks Dale "Did you really take pictures or not of us sleeping?" Dale answers "Well I did take one of you Tiff."

"What!" she yells, Dale explains "I'm sorry babe, but you were so cute. I just had to take one."

Tiffany replies "You better not show it anywhere to anyone."

Dale answers "I'm not going to. I'm going to frame it and set it on my nightstand, so when you're not with me in the mornings. You'll still, be the first thing I see when I wake up."

"Ahhh that's so sweat." Tiffany replied, and blows him a kiss

Becky says "That was sweat." She looks at Biff and continues "Old butt-head over here would never do something like that for me."

Biff responds "You got that right hoe." as he smiles.

"You son of a bitch" Becky replies, Biff chuckles and says to Dale "Man go on and park the car by the pump. All this sweat talking is making me gag."

as Dale parks, the car Biff turns his head toward Dale and says "You're so sweet, kiss, kiss, kiss, ya jerk off."

Dale responded "Dude chill."

Tiffany asks Biff "Why can't you be like that sometimes."

Biff answers "Because I'm not a lovesick puppy dog virgin, that's why." He steps out of the car and slams the door.

Dale rises out of the car and yells "Dude, what the hell that's all about?"

Biff answers "I'm sick of them always comparing me to you romantic pussy wiped dorks. Man you need to grow a pair."

"Dude!" Dale yelled.

As the guys continue outside the car, inside Tiffany says "Beck I'm sorry Biff is such an asshole."

Becky responds "Yeah, yeah me too."

Tiffany asks "Why do you stay with him anyway?"

Becky answers "I guess that's the only kind of guy that I can get. The assholes the only kind of guys I deserve." she finishes "Guys like Ray, and Dale, they don't go for girls like me. They can do a lot better than a girl like me."

Tiffany replies "Oh Beck you deserve better than that. There's a bunch of guys that would want you and treat you better than Biff."

Becky answers "Yeah, I know., I wish he was more like Ray, but he's all I got right now." Becky changes the subject by asking "What about you Tiff?"

Tiffany answers "What, what about me?"

Becky smiles asking "You, and Dale. why haven't you done it yet?"

Tiffany says "Oh, uh that, well, I'm not ready for that yet."

Becky replies "That's odd."

Tiffany asks "Why you say that?"

Becky explains "For someone who's ready to have kids, but not ready to do the deed with the guy she loves. Well, that sounds kind of odd."

"I Know." Tiffany replies "I just hope Dale is patience enough to wait til I am ready."

Becky answers "Don't keep him waiting too long. Them virgin balls of his are about to pop at the seam. You wouldn't want to find them inside any old easy body that comes alone now uh?"

Tiffany laughs "Haha, No, I wouldn't like that at all, haha."

Becky smiles saying "Hey, let's go to the restroom, then grab some snacks."

Tiffany answers "Okay." as they step out of the car Becky asks the guys "What are you two laughing about?"

Biff answers "We're just talking guy shit. You know how we are."

Becky replies "Yeah, we know how you are."

Tiffany adds "Yeah, we sure do."

The ladies headed for the store. Dale runs up to Tiffany and hands her some money as he speaks "This is for the gas, and this is to get you something with and get me a Chester Cola."

Tiffany responds "Okay, but don't you ever get tired, of drinking Chester Cola?"

As Dale is walking away from her he turns and answers with a smile "Never!"

Becky yells at Biff "Hey asshole you want something too!?" Biff yells back "Yeah, a good old fashion blow Job!"

Tiffany laughs as Becky sticks him the Bird.

Becky says "Let's go Tiff." then she mumbles "Dick head."

Minutes later as the Ladies leave the Bathroom and enters the Store.

As they're grabbing some snacks Becky notices the cashier behind the corner, she whispers to Tiffany

"Take a look at that big fellow."

Tiffany smiles as Becky continues "Look at those broad shoulders and his big strong arms. How would you like to get manhandled by that mountain of a man?"

Tiffany reacts "Beck. I didn't think you like, black guys."

Becky answers "Well I think some of them, are cute."

"Like Ray?" Tiffany asks

"Like Ray." Becky answered

Moments later they bring their items to the cashier he speaks

"Did you ladies find all you're looking for?"

Becky smiles and says "Not everything."

Tiffany jumps in saying "We're fine thank you."

Becky asks "How tall are you?"

He answers "About 6'5", 6'6"."

"Wow," Becky replies she asks, "You play football?"

He answers "Nah, it wouldn't be fair to the other players, I might hurt someone. I don't like hurting people."

they laugh.

He asks "You ladies passing through, or staying awhile?"

Tiffany answers "Passing through, we're on spring break, and we're headed for Gunther Beach."

Becky ask "And you big boy? You don't look like a local to me."

He answers "I've been here for a little while. It's a great little place to live when you want to get away from the hustle of the big world."

Becky asks "You got a name, what they call you big boy?"

He answers "M J."

"M J?" Becky asked

He adds "Not that M J." he looks at Tiffany and says "Not that M J either." He adds "Well ladies with the food, and gas your total comes to $32.92."

Moments later after the exchange, the girls are heading out the door, when Becky turns to ask M J

"Hey you got a number so I can call you when I'm in town again."

He answers "Just come to the store, I'm always here."

They smile at each other as she walks out the door

Tiffany whispers "I don't believe you did that?" Becky replies "What the big deal? I never get the good guys like that anyway. I get stuck with the assholes like Biff. And you know what? It's what I deserve."

Becky walks ahead with her head down, as Tiffany yells

"Beck! Becky! That's not true."

Meanwhile, the guys are back in the car Dale looks out the window he speaks

"Well here come the girls. You wonder what Beck said to the clerk?"

Biff answers "Hell no. I told you before, I don't care about this so-called relationship. To me, it's just a steady piece of ass. Because on this trip, I plan to get all the strange pieces of asses I can find."

Dale responds "You ready are, a dog."

Biff replies "Ruff, ruff."

Dale says "You talk like a pit, but you bark like a mutt."

Biff answers "Yeah, well, at least my balls are not about to explode from dryness hahaha."

Dale asks "Why did you say that to me? People keep saying things like that to me?"

The back doors open and the girls get in SLAM! As Tiffany hands Dale his cola,

She asks "You guys missed us?

Dale answers "Yeah babe, I was counting the minutes."

Biff turned from everyone and says "Yeah I missed you, like a nut shot that missed its target."

Tiffany sat back in the seat and says "That's gross." leaned forward and says "You're such an ass!"

Biff replies "Yup, that's me, such an ass."

Dale opens his cola, he looks at Biff and says "Dude, just drive."

Biff responds "Now that, something I can do. Ladies and Virgin, we're on the road again!"

as they leave the store parking lot Biff says to Dale "Oh you really should stop drinking that shit." Dale answers "Never."

<u>*Meanwhile, at Pookie's Dorm Room*</u>

Ray walks up to the room door he thinks to himself *"Hey why is Pook's door cracked open?"*

He walks in and yells out "Yo, yo Pookie!", "Yo Pook!" "Come on Pook, we're already late!"

He thinks to himself as he looks around *"Something wrong."* He speaks out louder "Dammit Pookie, what you got yourself into this time?"

He sits at the edge of Pookie's bed and thinks as he looks over the room.

"Come on Pook, you must have left a note, a clue or something."

He starts to focus on the video recorder on top of the TV.

"Hey Pook's recorder is on."

He jumps off the bed, grabs the camera and thinks,

"It's been recording all this time. Well, let's see what happened before I got here.

Good old Pook I knew you would leave some kind of a message."

Ray watched the video and yells as he runs out of the room "Dammit Pookie!"

An hour or two later
in the School Parking Lot

Donna is sitting in Ray's car she thinks to herself,
"How could I let Ray talk me into waiting in the car til he and Pookie gets here, It's been about two hours. I'm tired of waiting."

Just then Ray jumps in the front driver seat as Pookie jumps in the back.

Donna yells "Ray Ray!"

They hug Ray asks "You miss me Baby girl?" they kiss.

Pookie thinks *"Oh brother."* he puts his hand between them, so they would pull back from each other and says "Can you two spend five minutes together without locking

lips?, Gees."

Donna asks "Well? What Happened?"

Ray answers "Old Gangster Lean here almost got iced by some real street hoods."

"Yeah well I had everything under control until Action Jackson here came in with a fake gun talking about put 'em up, put 'em up!" Pookie replies, he adds, "Girl you should've

seen him. I cried, laughing."

"Ray!" Donna reacts,

Ray calmly says to Donna "That's not what happened."

Pookie Yells "Yeah you did, and if Big Joe didn't laugh his ass off, we both would be in body bags right now. Woo, girl you should've seen him."

Ray says to Donna "That didn't happen like that." "Let's get moving. Maybe we can catch up with the guys before they reach the beach."

Still laughing Pookie replies "Unless they've taken long rest stops, and you burn some serious rubber we're not gonna catch

them before they get there."

Ray responds "Yeah, we should be halfway there by now, but no your ass can't stay out of trouble."

Still laughing Pookie replies "Ah no, don't put that shit on me. No one told your simple ass to try to find me, talking about put em up, put em up. Hahaha woo, girl, you should've seen him."

As they drive from the parking lot Donna

says "Shut up Pookie."

Chapter 3
Welcome to Goodwind

After three hours of driving Biff finds himself in a bit of a daze, Dale notices and says,

"Hey man, dude, dude wake up." as he pokes his elbow into Biff's side.

Biff responds "Uh, oh, oh yeah I'm awake." as he yawns.

Dale says, "Alright dude, I think it's time for me to take the wheel. So park it."

Biff answers "Yeah Virgin I think you're right. Just let me find a good spot to change over."

Becky speaks up "Hey guys. Why don't we just stop at the next town and freshen up, and maybe get something to eat?"

Tiffany adds "Hey that sounds great."

Biff responds "That sounds like a plan to me ladies. "Yo D, what's the next town coming up?"

Dale looks at the highways signs "Uh, Goodwind, the town of Goodwind is up on the next exit." Dale reports, "How does that sound?

The girls answers "Yes, yup!"

Biff reacts saying "Alright Goodwind here we come." as he turns onto the exit.

Dale reads a sign.

**"Welcome to Goodwind Texas,
not to be confused with
Goodwin Texas."**

Becky says "That says a lot."

Biff replies "Yeah, well who gives a shit we're stopping anyway."

Minutes later Tiffany speaks "Hey look there's a place to eat."

Dale reads the sign

"Stinky Bar and Grill."

Biff says "Well, you guys want some stinky or what?"

Dale answers "Yeah man let's check it out."

Biff asks "Ladies, what you say?"

Becky says "Go for it." and Tiffany "Uh hello, hungry."

Biff replies "Stinky it is." He pulls the car into the parking lot.

Minutes later The kids walk into the Bar, while standing at the entrance, they all seem to get the feeling that every pair of eyes in the place were on them, plus it also went completely silent, then all of a sudden everyone went back as they were before, talking, eating, drinking, laughing. the place is alive.

Dale says "Well that was weird."

"What?" Biff asked

"That eerie silence that we walked into." Dale answered

Tiffany adds, "Yeah it was like we walked into where we shouldn't have."

Becky says "Yeah I kinda feel we're out of place here."

Biff looks around and replies "Relax." as he walks toward a table "Don't worry let's just grab a table so we can get something to eat. You guys. What a bunch of dorks."

Becky responds "Fine."

As they sit Dale reminds Biff "You're being an asshole again."

Biff answers "Gee Dale, thanks."

Just then a man steps toward them and says "Hello my young friends. Welcome, welcome to Stinky Bar and Grill. I'm your host

Salmon "Stinky" Stinkmeijer." "Gentlemen, Ladies please, please enjoy your stay with us. Everything on the menu is highly regarded."

with a snap of his fingers he calls out "Sammy, Sammy please come take these lovely people's orders." and "By the way my young friends, first rounds of drinks are on me."

Biff responds "Well alright, now you're talking."

Tiffany says to Stinky "Thank you so

much. You're so kind." the others agree.

"No, no my friends." Stinky replied, "Thank you for coming and spending time at Stinky. Enjoy your drinks, enjoy your meal, and enjoy the atmosphere here at Stinky." He bows his head and walks toward another table of customers.

Biff says "Wow, now that's a character." The young lady Stinky called over to help them step over and introduces herself "Hello I'm Samantha. May I take your orders?" As they place their orders the man at a nearby table is watching and listening to everything that's going on with them.

Dale noticed and whispers "Hey guys look that old gus. He been eagle-eyeing us since we got here."

The others look over, Biff says "Oh he

has uh. I'll deal with this. "Hey buddy."

Becky grabs Biff's hand and says "Biff please don't." Biff smiles at Becky saying

"Alright. Whatever." he pulls a map out of his back pocket, opens and spreads It on the table, and begins to look it over.

The man introduces himself "Hello young ones I'm Davy. Davy Lockheart" "How are ye on this fine day."

Tiffany answers "We're fine thank you. How are you."

"Me?" he replies "I be well me lass. May I ask, where ye youngsters be heading off to?"

Biff speaks, "Wait, I thought we be in Texas mateys. Where the hell did this, pirate guy come from."

Tiffany whisper "Shut up Biff." Dale adds "Yeah, Jees dude." Becky just stares at him and thinks *"Dam Biff, sometimes I want to punch him in the mouth."*

Dale answers "Mr. Lockheart, sir. "We're on our way to Gunther's Beach."

Lockheart replies "Ah." "Gunther's a find vacation spot, that's she is. But it be getting late, ye youngsters should think bout spinning the night over there in Collegeville."

Collegeville?" Dale replies, Biff ask "What the hell is Collegeville?"

Samantha returns with some of their order, she interrupts "Collegeville is on the west side of town. It's where all the college kids go for spring and summer break."

Lockheart adds "Ye youngsters should stay a day or two and check it out." Samantha continues,

"Yeah there are clubs, bars, movie theaters, mini golf, bowling allies, shopping, restaurants, and more."

Dale responds "Wow!, That sounds awesome." the girls agree.

A voice from another nearby table jumped in saying "Yes and a few more miles west you'll come to Goodwind Lake." They have cabins, places for bar-be-ques, campfires, swimming, and fishing, plus they have jet skies. All for your summer fun." You, kids, should check it out."

Biff then asks "And you are?"

"Me? Oh, you kids can just call me Jake." he answered.

Dale, responds "Well mister Jake, that place does sound fun. Maybe we should..."

Biff interrupts "No way virgin. We're going to Gunther, and going by this map, we can save some time by hitting highway 166."

Just then all eyes in the bar are on them, as Samantha drops Tiffany's food on the floor "I'm sorry, I'm sorry, I'll bring you another plate." she pleaded

"It's Okay." Tiffany says as she gently reaches for Samantha's arm and smiles." Samantha smiles, then heads back to the kitchen.

Lockheart speaks "You kids do wanna be headed down 1-66 at night. Too dangerous. What ya be wanted to do is bed down for the night, then be getting you a fresh start in the morning."

Biff looks at him and answers "Na, I don't think so pops. We're headed for Gunther right after we eat."

Jake responds "In that case kid, you might what to stick to the main road. 166 is not the road to be on at night. Believe me when I tell you."

Biff smiles and replies "Well I'm sure we can handle it pops."

Both Jake and Lockheart drop and shake their heads "Fucking kids." they both whispered.

The kids hear another voice "You kids should listen to your elders." the kids jumped as they looked up to see who the voice was, Becky remarks "You people just seem to pop

up out of nowhere don't you."

"Sorry, little lady, I didn't mean to startle

you, kids. I'm Sheriff Buckley."

Dale speaks "Well sheriff. What can we do for you?"

Buckley answers "Well for starters you kids can listen to good ole Jake, and Davy." "Route 166 is not the safest way to go between 6 pm and 6 am."

Biff replies "Yeah, well alright then." Tiffany looks at Biff and says "Biff maybe we should listen to them. I mean they do live here, they should know what they're talking about."

Buckley responds "Smart girl, you should listen to her sport."

Biff thinks to himself *This isn't going anywhere.* He answers "Maybe you're right sheriff, I think we will spend the night at your

Collegeville."

Buckley walks over to Biff put his hand on his shoulder and says "Smart move Sport." then he tips his hat to everyone and heads for the bar.

Dale says to Biff "This might be fun. Let's stay by the lake." The girls agree with Dale.

Biff drops his head starts to eat and only answers "Ah yeah uh hum."

Over at the bar as Buckley sits down the bartender pours him a drink, and lend in close and whispers "What you think Sheriff? Are they gonna stay the night?"

Buckley takes a drink then answers "Hell no. With Sport over there leading them. We might as well get the body bags ready."

The bartender replies "What we're gonna do Sheriff? You know what's ahead for these ids if they drive on 166."

"I know Pete, I know. But what we're gonna do? We can't tell them to much and warn them directly. The last person did that die the next day. Remember?"

"Yeah well, sheriff we have to do sometime."

"There's nothing we can do Pete, Unless your gonna tell them what their driving into." "Well?" the Bartender drops his head as Buckley finishes "I didn't think so Pete." He finishes his drink.

Back at the kids' table, Dale asks Tiffany "Hey what's with you Tiff?"
she answers "Wha...What?"

He continues "You been staring off into space for the last few minutes. What is it?"

She replies, "Oh I was just looking at that giant picture on the wall over there." "I wonder who he is? It's as if he was looking down at us. Almost like he's watching over us."

Jake interrupts "Maybe he is little lady, maybe he is."

Lockheart jumps in saying "That there be Colonel Beatty."

Jake says "Yup The ole Colonel. Goodwind's own favorite son. Captain of the football, and baseball teams. He fought in the war."

Biff asks "War, what war?"

Lockheart answers "The Big One kid. Ya youngster be have it good these days because of men like him."

Jake agreed saying "And he was the best sheriff Goodwind ever had." "Eh don't tell

Buckley, I said that."

Biff says "Wow sounds like a swell guy."

Lockheart "That he was youngster, that he was."

Tiffany asks "Whatever happened to him?" both man scared to say, each looking at the other to see which one is going to answer her question.

Jake says "Well, there was some trouble on 166, so he mustered up a posse, and called down some of his old army buddies."

Lockheart adds "They called them

Beatty's Brigade."

Jake continues "Yes, and they went to investigate...and uh well."

"Well?" Tiffany asked, "What happened?"

Lockheart answers "Urban Legend, young lady, Urban Legend."

Tiffany replies "Wow that's something."

Biff intervenes "Hey guys if your done eating, then let's get a move on. We've been here way too long."

Dale says "alright, alright dude, let me run to the bathroom first."

A few minuets later as Dale is washing his hands in the restroom Samantha walks in

"Excuse me, uh, Samantha right? I think you're in the wrong bathroom."

"I'm not here to pee, I'm trying to warn you."

"Warn me? About what?"

she looks around saying "It's about Highway 166."

"Oh that, You don't have to worry, Biff changed his mind, we're heading for the Lake."

"No no, your friend hasn't changed his mind, I can tell by the sound of his voice." "He's gonna take you all down 166, and if you go it's not gonna be good."

"What is it about that road with you people anyway," he asked

"All I can tell you is that it's very dangerous at night. Please, please don't go."

Dale smiles saying "I think everything gonna be alright Samantha."

She drops her head and says, "If you go, keep driving and don't stop until you get to the next town Bryce City. If you run out of gas, stay in your car. If you do get out, please, please stay on the road. DO NOT STEP OFF IT."

He pauses for a moment then asks "Okay. Why do you care so much?"

she asks "You don't know?"

he shakes his head no, and she lends in close to Dale saying "Your girlfriend might not

know what she got, but I do." then she kisses him.

He thinks to himself

"Okay this doesn't happen to me regularly, I don't usually, go for redheads, but man she can kiss."

Samantha pulls back and smiles as she starts to blush, Dale speaks "Wow, That was nice." He smiles.

A few minutes later as Dale steps out of the restroom he runs right into Biff "Woe dude you almost ran me over. What's the hurry?" Biff asked.

Biff takes a look at the situation then says "Oh well, I won't tell Tiff."

Dale responds "Uh, Tell Tiff what?" Biff answers "Well first I won't tell her that I saw that Samantha girl sneaking out of the men's bathroom 10 seconds after you stepped out. And I won't tell her about the lipstick all over your face."

Dale reacts "What the. I can Explain." as he starts to rub his face.

Biff says "Dude don't sweat it, I'm proud of you." Biff lends close to Dale, and asks "Did she give you some? No! Still a virgin huh? Meet you at the car, haha." Biff lightly punches Dale on the shoulder and walks in the restroom.

Dale turns to a mirror on the wall and continues to rub off the lipstick, just then he

hears a voice from behind "Dale." he turns and yells "What!" he pauses "Ah Tiff I'm..."

She cuts him off as her eyes tears up "Why are you yelling at me? Why are you being so mean!?" she runs to the women's restroom.

Dale pleads "Tiff I didn't mean to..."

Becky says "Don't worry Casanova I'll talk

to her." as she heads for the restroom.

Moments later in the ladies' room, Tiffany is trying to hold back her tears as Becky tries to comfort her

"Tiff you know Dale didn't mean to yell at you. You startled him."

"I know Beck. I just don't like being yelled at." my parents used to yell at me all the time.

Tiffany has a flashback of her parents and

briefly relives some of the brutal and mean-spirited words said to her, over the years as she tried to hold back a flow of tears Becky tries to comfort her, but Tiffany snaps back and continues speaking.

"It hurts for me to be reminded of their mistreatment." "Beck. Why was he so jumpy anyway?"

Beck answers "I don't know Tiff, I just don't know." Becky rubs Tiffany's shoulder until she stops crying, Tiffany grabbed Becky's hand kissed it, and says,

"Thanks Beck your my very best friend."

"Tiff we're more than friends. We're sisters." Tiffany smile and replies "Sisters."

Moments later as Dale and the girls start to walk back to the car Biff is standing by the door with Buckley and Stinky

Biff asks "Oh uh sheriff. Which way to that College town you guys were telling us about?"

Buckley pointed "Westward, that a way Sport." Buckley tipped his hat and says, "See you around Sport."

Biff smile saying "Uh yeah, right, see you around." as Biff turns away Stinky yells out to the kids.

"Y'all come back now ya hear." Dale and the girls wave as they get in the car. Still, smiling and waving Stinky lend toward Buckley and asks

"What do you think Sheriff? They gonna stay the night.?"

"Hell nah, Stinky." Buckley answered "With Sport leading them. He gonna drive them straight to hell."

"Well sheriff, we can't just sit by and let them go, it's already after 6." Said Stinky

Buckley responds "Dam it Stink, it's out of our hands. You know you can't tell these smart ass kid anything nowadays. We tried to warn them the best we could. Hell we even build Collegeville to save these kids. And still some of them go anyway. There's nothing we can do now."

Meanwhile, as Biff sits in the car and slams the door he says "You guys ready to roll?"

the others react "Yes, Yes, Yeah dude let go." Becky yells out "I can't wait to get to the lake." Tiffany adds "Maybe we can check out the Mall first." Dale says "Yeah I can go for a cool swim. Is anyone up for skinny dipping?"

Tiffany responds "Not even." Becky replies "You're nasty D."

Biff speaks as he starts driving "We're not going to the lake." Becky reacts "What!, But you said…"

Biff cuts her off "I know what I said, I just said that so those old guys would leave us alone. I didn't see any point arguing with them."

Dale answers "Yeah, but Biff they said 166 is very dangerous this time of night."

Biff smiles at Dale and says "And who told you that? Some redheaded girl maybe?"

Dale looks away from Biff in silence,

Becky jumps in "Just about everyone in

the place sad it Bonehead."

Dale turns back to Biff and says "Yeah, dude. We should just grab a cabin for the night, and get a fresh start in the morning."

Biff Responds "Yeah, yeah cabins by the lake. Picture me in the middle of some ass, and we get rudely interrupted by an ax-craved psycho wearing a ski mask. Slasher movie anyone? Well, not me buddy."

Dale laughs "You've seen too many movies dude."

"Well, bite me virgin." Biff answered

Becky says "Gee Biff, you're such a

dickhead." Biff answers "That's me Mr. Dickhead." "Gunther Beach here we come."

Tiffany says, "Jees, are we there yet?"

As the kids drive off Buckley and Stinky continue their conversation

"Well there goes Sport and his band of doomed followers. Just like that woman, and her two kids a few weeks ago."

"Sheriff we got to do something."

Buckley answers "I am. I'm gonna get four body bags ready, five if Samantha said too much to the other boy."

"How...how much do you think she told him.?

"I don't know Stink, but we'll see in the morning. Hell you know how things works, you saw what happened to Frankie Lee a few weeks back, and Jessie May years ago. You say too much, and you're dead the next day."

"But sheriff..."

"But what Stink. Are you gonna hop in your car, catch them. If they stop, you then gonna tell them everything they're driving to. and after they're done laughing at you, they're still gonna keep going, and in the morning you'll be just as dead alongside them. If that's what you want, then go on ahead. Be my guess."

Stinky paused

Buckley finishes "Yeah Stink, that's what I

thought," he walks off,

Stinky thinks to herself *"This shit got to end, somehow, someway this shit got to end."* 7:08 pm

45

<u>Chapter 4</u>
The Beaten Path, Route 166

Biff announces "Alright boys, girls, and virgins too, we're about to get on 166 highway. Next stop Bryce City."

Tiffany asks "How long will it take to get there?"

Dale answers "According to the map about 40 minutes give or take."

Becky yawns and says, "Great well wake me when we get there." Tiffany adds, "Yeah, I'm beat too. I must have eaten too much."

Dale says, "Yeah old Stinky had some good food. We got to stop there again on the way back."

Biff looks over at Dale and says "On that Virgin we agree."

All of a sudden a bright blinding light flashes by "Woe!" Yelled Dale "What the hell was that?!"

Tiffany adds "Yeah I saw it too, what was that?"

"What was what?" Becky asked as well

Biff answers "A bright ass light got the Ladies and the Virgin panties all knotted up."

Dale responds "Okay fearless wonder you explain what the hell that was."

Biff answers "Well you see son, when Daddy photon and Mommy photon hook up they make a baby which we call light."

"That's not what I meant you prick." Dale replied "I mean what's that all about."

Biff answers "I don't know dude, it could've been a chopper or a low-flying plane."

"Low-flying plane my ass. What would a plane be flying that low flashing bright lights like that at this time of night for." Dale responded.

Biff answered, "I don't know, they're probably looking for the airstrip so they can land."

Dale Yells "Airstrip! Airstrip! I didn't see no airstrip on the map!"

"That's because you weren't looking for one, gees."

Becky says "Well I didn't see anything. I was trying to sleep, but I could feel that bright light on my face."

Tiffany says "I don't think that was a plane or a chopper. Maybe we should just turn around and go back to Goodwind."

Becky joins in saying "Yeah Biff maybe we should just turn back."

Biff reacts "Are you bitches shitting me? Are you bitches fucking shitting me right now?"

as the yelling back and forth continues Dale's mind fades out from the noise every word that is said sounds like blah, blah, blah to him at this moment. Then one voice breaks through the muddled mess.

It's Samantha's voice. She sounds so sweet and sensual, yet so blunt, and bold. "Her warnings!" he thinks to himself. He speaks "Guys, guys. Let's just keep going. Just drive til we get to Bryce City."

Biff responds "Well alright, finally a voice of reason."

Sometime later Dale asks "What time is it?"

Tiffany rises up, looks at her watch, and answers "Uh, it's about 9:15. How long did you say it would take to get to Bryce City?"

Biff answers "According to the map about 40 minutes."

Tiffany responds "40 minutes, Biff you've been driving for at least 2 hours."

Becky adds, "Feels like you been driving forever, Biff you're lost."

Biff responds "I'm not lost, the map's a little off, that's all." Tiffany looks out the window and notices "Hey there's a house. Let's stop and ask for directions."

Biff responds "Yeah Tiff, we'll just stop off at a creepy old house at night in the middle of nowhere Texas. You guys don't watch many horror movies do you."

Dale remembers Samantha's warnings. He jumps in saying "I'm with Biff on this one, let's just keep driving."

Becky says "Look there's another house." Tiffany replies "Looks like the same one we just passed a few miles back."

Dale answers "Must be the style around here." Biff agrees "Yeah must be."

11:20 pm

Biff breaks the last hour of silence by yelling "Okay now this is just ridiculous."

Becky responds "We told you we were lost hard-head." Biff answers "Shut up Beck! Just shut up!"

Dale turns to Biff "Hey man just keep driving okay, just keep driving."

Biff answers "I'm not gonna be driving for much longer, the gas is getting low."

Becky responds "Great, just great. We got to be close to somewhere by now."

"No, no we're right where we're meant to be." said Tiffany staring out the window.

Biff responds "What Tiff? What are you talking about?!" Becky rises her voice at Biff "Don't yell at her!" Biff replies "Then tell her to explain what she's talking about."

Tiffany answers "The map shows a trip that is 40 minutes tops, but we've been driving for hours now. Every few miles I keep seeing what appears to be the same house over and over again as if we're going in circles. We all saw an unexplained flash of light. Plus we're almost out of gas in the middle of nowhere."

Biff yells "What are you trying to say Tiff!? What are you trying to say!?"

Becky yells again "Don't yell at her!" Biff replies "Yeah well tell her to just say what's she's trying to say."

Tiffany thinks to herself *I'm not gonna let his yelling get the best of me, I'm gonna say what I need to say.* she speaks "All the people back in Goodwind tried to warn us that bad things happen on this road at night, but we didn't listen. You didn't listen Biff. You brought us here because you didn't want to listen, and we were stupid enough to follow you."

Biff looks at Dale and says "Virgin you better check your girl before I punch a new flavor in her mouth."

"Biff!" Becky yells "You won't lay a hand on her! Apologize to her!"

Biff responds "What! Oh hell I didn't mean it Tiff. But don't go putting all this on my shoulders. Like you said you guys didn't have to follow me." He pause, He asks "A little help virgin?"

Dale says "Everybody just chill, and you, asshole just keep driving." Biff answers "No way virgin, this car is about to spit out its last bit of juice."

The car starts to sputter a little, it makes a knocking sound glides a few feet, and comes to a complete stop. Biff turns toward the girls and says "This bitch is dead.

49

Meanwhile

Ray, Donna, and Pookie are still playing catch-up with the others. Donna is fast asleep until her head slips from her arm in which the sudden jerking movement causes her to snap awake, she gathers herself, looks towards Ray, and asks "What time is it, baby?"

He answers "Oh, oh so you're awake now. It's...uh 11:30 baby girl." I'm glad to finally have some company."

Pookie speaks "You had some company, but your punk ass told me to shut the hell up about 3 miles back."

Donna says "Pookie don't start."

He replies "Start what I was just...You know what I got to pee. Can we stop somewhere?"

Donna agrees "Yeah Ray baby. I could use a little freshening up myself."

Ray answers "That's cool, I was planning on finding a spot to gas up anyway. I'll take this next exit coming up. Then we can get a map and see if we can find a shortcut, and catch the others."

as they switch on to the exit Pookie reads the sign

"Goodwind. Have you guys ever heard of Goodwind Texas? Well have you?"

Ray answers "Uh no Pook, Can't say I have."

Donna agrees "Me either, never heard of it."

Pookie replies "Exactly. Small nowhere town, late at night, on a road trip."

Donna asks "And?"

Pookie continues "And! That doesn't sound like a horror flick to you? Hills with Eyes, Dust to Dawn, Scooby-Doo, and a whole lot of other scary shit like that?! Huh? You guys don't see that?!

Ray chuckles saying, "Lighten up Pook. Those are just movies."

Pookie replies "Movies my ass! Art imitates life mother..."

"Hey look at that sign." Donna said as she cuts Pookie off, she reads

"Welcome to Goodwind Texas,

not to be confused with

Goodwin Texas.

Wow now that's a mouth full."

Pookie shakes his head and says "It's Halloween all over this. Friday the 13th. House of Wax. It's over. Game over. Thanks for playing. Do not pass go."

NIGHT ON THE HAUNTED HIGHWAY

Ray yells "Pookie! "Shut the Hell up!"

12:45 Back on 166

Biff and the others are walking down the road Becky yells out "Oh!, My feet hurt. Why did we get out of the car anyway?"

Dale answers, "Ask fearless leader, I said we should've stayed in the car."

Biff jumped in, "And stay in the car all night? Yeah right virgin."

Dale responds "Dude I getting tired of you calling me that. I'm willing to let a few jabs slide, but you're taking things too far, and it's getting old Biff."

Biff replies "Calm down, calm down don't get your panties all knotted up." "I'm Just..."

Dale interrupts "Hold on, wait a minute." He thinks *Is that what I think it is?* He yells, "It is!" He runs laughing.

Biff Yells, "Dam dude what the hell wrong with you!?" Biff starts running after him as the girls follows, them both yelling for the guys to stop.

As Dale slows down Biff yells, "What the deal dude?" Becky asks "What going Dale?" "Yeah Baby what's up?" Tiffany asks.

Dale answers, "This red box, it's a phone."

Biff asks, "Who would put a phone in the middle of nowhere."

Dale answers "It's an emergency phone meathead."

Biff asks, "Why would they put a phone on the side of the road?"

Becky answers, "Biff shut up!"

Tiffany says, "We can call for help."

Biff smile saying, "Well don't call Sheriff Buckley, that chicken shit rent-a-cop won't be coming out here this time of night.

Dale opens the box, grabs the phone, and smiles as he starts to dial "We're good now." the phone sounds off

"BEEP, BEEP, BEEP,

I'm sorry, but this unit

is no longer in service."

Dale Yells "No! No! No! Hell no!" "It's out of order."

Biff shakes his head saying "Dam. Anymore bright ideals virgin?"

Becky refuse to give up as she grabs the phone "It can't be." she dials, it sounds off

"BEEP, BEEP, BEEP,
I'm sorry, but you
should not have come here
Bitch."

She screams "What the hell!"

Tiffany asks "Becky what's wrong?" Biff asks, "Dam girl you lost your mind, or what?" Dale noticed "Biff she's shaking all over." "Beck, Becky what happen did you hear someone?"

Becky starts to calm down as she answers "It's nothing, yeah it's nothing. I'm just tripping."

Biff grabs the phone he dials, it echos,

"BEEP, BEEP, BEEP,
I'm sorry, but this unit
is no longer in service."

He looks at Becky "Yeah girl, you're tripping." He looks at Dale "You got anymore bright ideals virgin?"

Dale replies "Well, I can bash this phone across your forehead." Biff responds "Dream on you puss..."

Tiffany interrupts "Look guys there's a house maybe we can ask the people there for some help."

Becky says "It's about time we get to another house."

Tiffany answers "It's not another house. It's the same house we been passing all night."

"Bullshit!" Biff reacted, "Tiff you're one crazy bitch, you know that."

"You know Biff, it's bad enough you give me and Beck a lot of grief, but I'll be dammed if you think I'm gonna let you talk to Tiff like that." Dale said as he squares up to Biff.

A brief stare down then Biff answers back "Oh look ladies, what you're witnessing before your very eyes, a virgin about to grow his balls, take notes ladies this is a rear event."

"You know what Biff, the hell with you."

"Don't you turn your back on me!" Biff yells as he punches Dale in the back of his head knocking him off his feet, Dale uses his hands to break his fall so his face doesn't hit the pavement, Dale turns over as Biff steps over him,

"I should kick your virgin ass right here and now, virgin boy."

Dale answers back "Not tonight Biff." as he thrust his leg forward kicking Biff in his knee, which forces him back a few steps.

Dale jumps to his feet and as the two-step toward each other Becky steps between them with her hands out trying to keep them from each other "Guys, guys don't fight, we've been friends way too long for this."

Tiffany speaks "Hey guys look there's a light on in the house."

"So what?" Biff asked

"Yeah what about it." Becky asked,

"All the lights were off when I first saw the house." Tiffany answered,

"And?" Dale asked

"And that could mean someone is up and may be able to help us out." she explained

as everyone just looked at each other Biff extended his hand to Dale asking "Truce?" Dale agrees "Truce." they shake hands.

Biff says "Okay the house it is." he looks toward the girls, smiles saying, "Ladies first." As they start walking toward the house Biff says "You know I wasn't gonna fight you for reals." Dale says, "Really?

Biff answers, "Yeah man your a virgin. There's laws against harming endangered species."

Dale laughs "Biff shut the fuck up."

Meanwhile Back in Goodwind

Ray, Donna, and Pookie are about to get on 166, as they do, a FLASH of light beams down over them. Pookie ask "What the hell was that?"

"What was what?" Ray asked,

"So you're trying to tell me that you didn't see that bright ass flash of light just now? Really, really!"

"Yeah, babe. What was that?" Donna asked,

Ray, answers "Uh, well I don't know a low-flying plane maybe."

"Wait what?" said Pookie "A low-flying plane. You're trying to tell me that was a low-flying plane. Ray stop talking, just stop talking, a low-flying plane this late at night, in the middle of nowhere. A low-flying plane. Are you shitting me Ray? What happened is we just drove into some kind of Twilight Zone bullshit. Low-flying plane."

"Pook will you just give it a rest! Everything's fine." Ray yelled,

Pookie responds "Everything's fine he says, I knew I should've listened to that sexy redhead back at the store. She said some bad shit was gonna go down if we drove here tonight, but noooo, you wanted a shortcut so you could catch with your boy Biff, I should've just stayed with her got me some loving, and live to talk about it in the morning, but nah, we're gonna die, I can see it...I can see it."

"Will you just stop it Pookie DAM!" Yelled Donna.

Ray yells "You know Pook you can just get out and walk your ass back to the store, and be with your new girlfriend."

Pookie chuckles saying "She also said not to get out of the car, dumb ass."

Donna replies "Pookie, shut up, just please shut the hell up."

<u>Chapter 5</u>

That Old House to the Right

Meanwhile, as Biff and the others walk onto the house property Dale thinks to himself as he slaps his forehead, *"Dammit Samantha said to stay on the road if we got out, the car."* he speaks out loud "Well I guess we're no longer following the Yellow Brick Road Dorothy."

Biff says "What? What the hell you're talking about dude?"

"Oh, uh nothing, just an old movie my grandparents would watch,"

Biff replies "Ha,...Right, whatever man."

as the youngsters are about to step onto the front porch Dale looks to his right and yells "What the hell!"

Biff responds "What, what is it dude?"

Dale was somewhat frozen as he tries to process what he saw, Biff places his hands on Dale's shoulders, shaking him and saying, "Dude, dude what is it."

Dale snapped back and looks Biff in the eyes saying, "I saw,... There was,... Someone or something was peeking around the house looking at us."

Becky and Tiffany started to move closer to the guys shaking,

Becky asks "What was it?" Tiffany asks "Are you sure you saw something?"

Dale answers "I'm sure."

Biff focuses on Dale and asks "Could you make out what it was, can you describe him?

Dale answers, "No, all I could see was a dark figure,...it ducked back around the corner just when I looked in it's direction.

I only saw it for a split second."

Biff smile saying, "Relax dude. It was probably a dog or something."

Dale responds "A dog Biff. Yeah a dog. Must be one of those tall two-legged kind."

Biff smiles saying, "Enough." he walk toward the front door and says "Ladies. One of you gonna ring the bell before whoever up goes back to bed?

Forget it I'll do it." the girls answered

as Biff is about to ring the bell

Tiffany stops him and says, "Biff careful there may be others that still trying to sleep."

"Yeah, Biff." Becky adds "Try to be a gentleman."

Biff looks at Becky and winks, as he answers, "Gentlemen? and ruin your image of me."

Just then Dale looks to his left and yells "What the hell!"

Biff asks "What with you man?"

Dale answers, "I saw it again, it was looking right at us again. it's was on the other side of the house."

Biff says, "It was probably some kids."

Dale reacts "Kids? Kids at 2:00am in the morning."

Biff replies "Maybe it's a neighbor, I don't know."

Dale reacts "Neighbor. What neighbor this is the only house for miles."

Biff says, "Look man I don't know what you saw okay. Just stop it you're frightening the girls."

Becky adds "Yeah Dale cut it out."

Dale drops his head, looks dead into Biff's eyes saying, "Fine, I'm gonna see who, or what that is."

"What Biff asked,

Dale continues "I'm gonna go around the house to the left. Why don't you go around to the right, then whatever it is we can catch it in the middle." Dale pauses waiting for an answer he says, "Whatever Biff I'm going."

As Dale started to walk off biff grabbed his arm saying, "Woo, woo, woo, hold on Dale. Now wait a minute, you just don't watch horror movies at all do you."

Dale answers "What!"

Biff explains "Horror movie 101. Never split up. No matter what, we stay together right?" He turns to the girls and asks, "Right ladies?"

the ladies agree "Yeah, sure we stay together." "Together forever."

Biff turns back to Dale and ask "Well?"

Dale answers "Whatever, together."

Biff smiles, they shake hands. Biff says to the girls, "Will one of you please ring the bell, and see if we can get some help."

Becky rings the bell, RING! RING! She rings it again RING! RING! She says, "I think I heard someone moving."

Tiffany yells "Hello! Hello, can you help us?! We're lost, and our car ran out of gas!" "Can you please, please help us!"

After a moment of silence Biff speaks "Uh, well maybe we should...."

just then the door opens "Hello?" said Tiffany,

Dale speaks "Okay I don't see anyone, so, uh did the door just opened by itself?"

Becky asks "What do we do just walk on in?"

Biff answers, "Uh, yeah, yeah let's go in. Me first, Dale you bring up the rear." as the kids walk into the house they hear a voice

"Greeting young ones, welcome."

Dale says "Who said that?"

They see at the end of the living room a short figure, Biff says, "Oh it was the little old lady over there." the old lady smiles saying,

"My my, what sweet and tender youngsters you are. What can Mother do for you dears?"

Biff says, "Ha, sweet and tender, ha right. Nothing to worry about here."

Becky elbowed Biff saying, "Shut up Biff. Hello mam, we're lost and out of gas."

Tiffany adds "Can you help us? May we use your phone?"

The old lady placed her hand on her forehead and says,

"My phone? Oh yes, my phone. It's in the parlor. But you sweet tarts should freshen up first."

She looked around and called out,

"Clifford!"

a heavy bass voice speaks out right next to the kids

"Yes madam?"

The kids all jumped as they were startled.

Dale asks "So we just gonna act like this tall ass Frankenberry-looking dude didn't just come out of nowhere, right?"

Tiffany responds "Shh Dale be nice." the old lady speaks,

"Clifford will show you to your rooms so you can freshen up. Then he will take you to the parlor to use the phone."

The kids all looked at Clifford Biff says "My, my Clifford, you're a big fellow. Dale I think we've solved your mystery from outside."

Dale answers "I don't think so Biff." Dale turns to speak to the old lady but he yells to the others "What the hell! The old lady's gone."

Biff answers "What, where did she go?"

Dale says "It's like she just disappeared out of thin air."

Becky responds "Oh she probably just went up the stairs."

Dale replies "You mean the stairs that weren't there earlier right."

Tiffany says "Guys you're scaring me."

Clifford speaks,

"This way sirs, Ladies."

Biff says "The old lady must be a ninja or something. Hum... Lead on Jeeves." as he pats Clifford on the shoulders.

As they all walk through a massive hallway

Biff whispers, "Wow, this place is huge."

Dale whispers "I don't remember the house looking this big from the outside., Do you Biff?"

Becky whispers "Guy please stop it. I'm creeped out enough as it is walking down this scary hallway, And with all those pictures of people looking down at us."

Tiffany whispers "Look at that picture there. That's the soldier sheriff. That's the same picture we saw back at stinky."

Dale responds "Yeah babe you're right how could there be the same picture here?"

Clifford who heard every word whispered turn back to the kids and says **"The solider-sheriff was highly regarded in this county. There are not many homes around here that don't have this picture of him. He was so much loved."** he turns forward and says **"Come along young tenders."**

Biff whispers "Well that explains the picture, But I'm not gonna get used to being called Tender."

As they continue down the hallway Becky tries to grab hold of Biff's hand, but he keeps pushing her hand away, she thinks to herself *"I'm so afraid right now and he won't even hold my hand, He doesn't care about me at all."* as her eyes start to tear up the eerie silence is broken when Tiffany speaks

"So Mr. Clifford, who are all these people in the photos."

Clifford answers **"Why young madam, they are mostly friends and family of the masters of the house."**

Tiffany asks "What about that one. How come that frame doesn't have a picture in it?"

Clifford answers **"Dear child that one belongs to a lost member of the family."**

"Lost member?" she asked

"Yes, yes, some would say the Black sheep, every family has that one.

he stops and looks at Dale then grabs his shoulder, saying, **"Your room sir."**

Dale says "Dam Clifford you got a hell of a grip, you guys don't want to arm wrestler this guy."

Clifford places Dale into the room and says **"Bathroom to the right, closet with fresh clothes to the left."** as he starts to close the door Dale grabs it saying,

"Hey wait a minute, we're supposed to stay together guys remember."

Biff looks at Dale and says "It's okay dude. Let's just do as they say, and we'll all meet up at the parlor."

Biff and Dale nodded at each other as Clifford closed the door. Dale looks around the room saying "Horror movies 101 my ass."

As the others continue, so does Tiffany as she notices yet another odd thing about the pictures,

"Hey Clifford all but one picture has only one person, but why that one has three people? Looks like a mother and her two kids."

He answers **"Ah yes young madam, they are the newest members of the master's family."**

She replies, "Newest members. They look like I've seen them somewhere before."

He answers, **"Surely not young madam. They don't get out much."** he stops and opens a door for Becky saying, **"Your room Madam."**

Becky looks at Biff, he gives her a head juster to go in, she does, Clifford closes the door. Becky starts to cry.

A few moments later as they arrive at the next room Clifford looks at Biff saying, **"Your room sir."**

Biff responds as he walks in "My room uh. Oh by the way Jeeves. What time is tea?, And will there be crumpets as well."

as Clifford starts to close the door as he answers **"Good one sir."**

once the door closed he addresses Tiffany **"This way madam."** as they continue down the hallway.

<u>Biff's Room</u>

Biff wondered to himself *"How the hell we're gonna get out of this? I wonder if that old lady has a sexy granddaughter, or something?*

<u>Dale's room</u>

Dale thinks to himself *"I wonder when we're gonna get to the parlor. This is starting to feel...."* Just then a voice speaks to him **"Hello cutie. How are you sweet."**

Dale jumps as he sees a young, beautiful woman, he yells, "Where the hell you come from?!"

She answers, **"I've been here the whole time."**

"Really?" he asked.

"Yes, and I been waiting for you for a long time."

He replies "You have? Who. Who are you?"

"I'm whomever you want me to be. And I'm here to take your virginity." she said as her body changes into someone that he is more familiar with.

He looks at her saying "Stacy?"

<u>Becky's room</u>

She has just stopped crying, now fear starts to set in "I'm so scared, I don't know what to do. We shouldn't split up."

She hears a voice saying ***"No need to fear, I'm here."***

she looks and sees "Ray, Ray!" she yells, "How, did you get here so fast, I mean you guys were hours behind us, right."

He answers ***"Shoot girl I've been here, waiting on you girl the whole time."***

"Ha, what, what are you talking about Ray?"

I'm talking us girl, me and you."

"What?" she asked,

he answers ***"Come on girl you know it's all about me, and you."***

"But where's Donna, and Pookie?" she asked

"Let's not talk about them right now." music starts to play as he claps his hands, he reaches for her hand saying, ***"Come on girl let's dance."***

<u>Biff's room</u>

He's laying on the bed thinking *"Ugh we should've been at the beach long by now. Shit, I should be up to my neck with some fine asses. But no, I had to get trapped here at the Bates Motel." "How long do old Cliff think it will take for us to freshen up? I beginning to think that something just ain't right. Maybe we shouldn't have split up. Some fearless leader I turned out to be. Dam I'm such an asshole."*

The Hallway

Tiffany continues walking with Clifford "Well it's looks like the end of the pictures coming up." she remarked

"**Yes.**" Clifford answered

Tiffany stop and start to focus in on the last few and says "These last ones are just empty frames. Why you got them up?"

Clifford's voice begins to fade as he answers **"Oh young tender those are for the newest members of the family to come, hahaha!"**

She ponders his words "Newest members of the family? "Hmm four empty frames, and four of us. Wait a minute Cliff?" as she turns to confront him she is shocked "Clifford!, Clifford!!, Where the hell did he go, Clifford!!!" almost to the edge of tears she thinks *"Oh crap, oh crap, Dale where are you, I'm so scared.*

Just then she hears "Uh, crying?" she turned toward the end of the hallway she sees *"Ah it's a little girl."* she thought "Hey little one, hey don't cry. What's wrong baby?"

The little girl with her back towards Tiffany raised her head and smile.

Meanwhile Back on the highway

Ray, Donna, and Pookie are still riding along "Dig dig dig dig-dig dig dig dig." the eerie tone Pookie continues to sing for the last hour or so until Ray finally interrupts "Pook, Pook, will you stop with that noise man!"

Donna asks "What's that about anyway Pookie?"

He replies "I don't know. Imagine three fools on a late night road trip. On a stretch of road that's only 40 minutes long, yet they been driving for 3 hours plus."

"Okay stop it Pookie." Donna replies, but he continues

"Traveling through what appeared to be some kind of a light barrier."

"Stop it Pookie." she repeats

He continues "Yes my friends for these three fools have just entered... The Twilight Zone. Dom! Dom! Dom!"

"Alight Pookie that's enough! What the hell Dude? You're scaring Donna!" Ray Yelled

Pookie goes off "You're yelling at me Ray" "I was trying to get you guys to stay back in Goodwind."

Ray answers "You were trying to get laid Pookie."

Pookie replies "Yeah, that too, but at least we weren't gonna get served up on an all-you-can-eat soul food platter."

"Pookie Stop it!!" Donna yelled

"Okay, okay." Pookie replies, a short pause then "Dig, dig, dig, dig." Both Ray, and Donna yells "Shut the hell up Pookie!!!"

Back at the house,
Dale's Room

He asks, "Stacy how in the world are you here?"

"I told you, I can be whoever you want me to be." she answered **"If this, is not the one you want."** as she changes her look again **"How about some dark meat?"** she concludes

Now even more shocked "Mary? Mary Maryland? How can this be?" he asked

she says as she changes again **"Or maybe you want the fiery redhead to give you the sex your girlfriend will never give you?"**

"Samantha? He asked

She grabs him, presses him to her body, kisses him, a long and passion kiss, rubbing her hands all over his body parts that Tiffany would never touch.

He thinks to himself _"Oh shit! I'm gonna get laid."_

Becky's room

She, and Ray are slow dancing not once did she think to even ask where the music was coming from, for she's in total bliss as she starts to feel the passion, the tenderness that she always wanted. All the pain of watching Donna get the full loving attention that she always wanted to receive has now faded.

He begins to kiss along her neck, ear lobe, as she smiles and closes her eyes.

"Oh Ray, oh Ray." she pants as he replies

"Oh yes, oh yes." steadily kissing her between every word he speaks.

Just then the thought hits her, she stops and stares it him saying "Donna's my friend, Biff's your friend. What about them?

He responds **"I told you let's not talk about them."** He takes her hand and gently turns her around, so he can grab hold of her from behind, wrapping his arms all around her. She closes her eyes again and leans her head back as she can feel the warmth of his passion against her body. He rubs the side of his face to hers as he says

"I want you!"

She answers "Take me Ray. Take all of me." She continues to move her body to the music with his, still with her eyes closed, fully enjoying the moment.

Ray lean his head back, opens his mouth, and out comes a long beastly looking tongue dripping with some kind of reddish, and greenish goo. As if it had a mind of its own, it begins to lick up and down her neck making her feel even more passion than she ever felt before.

He speaks gently, **"Sweet Tender."**

Biff's room

He has been sleeping for the last few minutes but is awakened when he feels his legs being touched. He rises, quickly to see what was going on. He sees two young beauties giggling as they kept rubbing his legs.

"Well, well, well, hello ladies. Where did you cuties come from?" he started to reach out and touch them and do so rubbing himself. Both still giggling as he asks

"So you ladies have names or what?"

The blond answers **"I'm Mee."** and the brunette says **"I'm Myy."**

Biff responds "Oh me, oh my, you two are, Woo!" he looks towards the front door and sees two more girls.

"Oh wow! Some more cuties. Hello ladies." he said as he jumps up to meet them "And you are?" he asked

"I'm Bee." said one, **"And I'm Dee."** said the other

Biff smiles saying "A redhead, and a sister. Okay, okay, I'm liking this." and as he starts rubbing the two newbies, he notices two more ladies standing by the bathroom door. "Oh my, two more cuties, this is a real party now." he heads toward them asking, "Who are we adding to our roster now?"

one says **"I'm Le."** and the other says **"I Ana."**

Biff responds "Oh yes, Asian, and Latino. All my favorite favors." All the ladies giggle as they all come up to him rubbing their hands all over his body. he's caught up in all of the many comments he's hearing from them

"Oh baby., He some sweet., Can't wait to taste him. And so young, so strong, so tender. Yeah."

Overwhelmed by all the praise, he waves his hands saying "Hold on, hold on. Ladies, ladies please. There's plenty of me to go around." "But first ladies I'm gonna give you a sample of what's on the menu." He takes off his shirt and begins to flex as the girls giggle, and cheer him on. As he continues posing he thinks to himself *"Yeah I'm gonna have me some fun tonight."*

One of the ladies whispers **"Tender's Sweet."** the other agrees.

Back in the Hallway

Tiffany is still trying to console the little girl "Hey little one don't cry. My name is Tiffany. What's yours?"

The little girl stopped crying, turns around, stares at Tiffany for a moment, turns back and starts to cry again.

Tiffany noticed, *"That's the girl in the picture.".* She asks, "Hey is that you with your mommy and brother in the picture."

The girl answers, while holding back her tears **"Yes."**

Tiffany asks, "Where, where are they?"

The girl answers, **"They're gone. My mommy is gone, and I have no mommy."**

Tiffany thinks, *"Poor thing."* as her eyes begin to tear up, "I'm so, so sorry about your mommy."

The girl stopped crying a large smile came to her as she asks, **"Will you be my mommy?"**

Tiffany froze for a moment as the girl's words were like music to her ears as she desperately wanted to hear the voice of a child calling her mommy.

Tiffany answers, with tears in her eyes "Yes, oh yea I would love to be your mommy."

The girl raised her head her eyes starts to glow, she lick her lips as she says, in a monstrous voice **"I was hoping you said that!"** she turns to Tiffany yelling, **"Sweet Mommy, sweet mommy!"** as she charges Tiffany.

Seeing the little monster attacking her Tiffany yells, "What the hell are you?! Those teeth, that tongue!! Get away from me!!"

she kicks the girl as hard as she could, the girl hits the wall and landed on the floor laying on her stomach, the girl opens her eyes as she speak in her little girl voice

"Mommy kicked me. Why mommy? Why mommy kicked me?"

Still somewhat stunned Tiffany pauses for a moment as she thinks, *"What just happened? But I thought. How could I? What is wrong with me? But those long sharp teeth, and that hideous tongue, I must be seeing things."*

She snaps out of her thoughts as she hears the little girl cry again. She remakes "What have I done."

Biff's Room

He's still putting on a show flexing for the lovely ladies boasting with each flex as they continue cheering him on "All right ladies time to show you the full package." as he turns around to show off his backside, all the ladies fell silence "Okay, ladies, like I said there's enough of me to go around. The question is. Who's first?"

He turns back to face them "Dam!! You bitches got some long pointy teeth, and what's up with those slimy green tongues!" he starts to back away from them as they slowly start to creep toward him

"Uh you know what, there's really not enough of me to uh, go around, so I'm just gonna go out and get my friend Dale, and I'll be back, with uh, Dale and uh, we're gonna show you ladies, uh things a, uh good time. Yeah, yeah a really good time."

he continues to ease toward the door, but every word from him seems to make the girly things mouth's drool more and more.

The standoff gets more intense as he can see the hunger in their reddish-greenish eyes "Well it's not the way I plan my vacation to go, but if I'm going down. It won't be without a fight! Ladies like I said earlier. Who's first!"

He yells as the lead girly thing yells, **"Sweet Tender!!!"** they rush him, he throws a punch "Take that bitch!" he yells as he strikes the lead thing knocking it to the floor, but the others are just too many to overcome as they forced him to the floor, with his back pinned against the door. They begin to bite and tear chucks from his body as he sits on the floor propped up against the door, he thinks, *"Oh shit, oh shit! These bitches are eating me alive. Ouch, oh please stop please!"* he starts to throw another punch until he notices, *"Wow my arms are gone. That black chick is eating one of them, I don't see the other. Oh, oh it hurts so bad, hey look the redhead, and the blond are fighting over my leg, ha I wonder which one? Oh, oh please get this over with it hurts so bad. Oh wow, that one's eating my heart. it's so small, no wonder I gave Beck so much shit., I wish I could see her again, tell her, tell her..."*

He speaks out loud "Becky!, if you can hear me, I, I, love, u..." As his last words are spoken he fades into the darkness with the things continuing to devour what's left of him. The smacking of lips, and the satisfaction of a great meal. The last words ring out from the room. **"Sweet Tender, sweet tender, sweet tender!**

Back in the Hallway

Still feeling bad for kicking the little girl Tiffany continues trying to comfort her in hopes that she will stop crying.

"It's alright, I didn't mean to hurt you. Come on, it's okay. You can stop crying, mommy's here now." she said as she slowly reaches for the child.

The little girl turns yelling monstrously, **"Mommy!"** With it's long pointed teeth bits Tiffany's hand ripped off pieces of her pinkie, and ring figures.

Tiffany screams "You Little Bitch!!" She kicks the girl thing even harder than the first time. Tiffany clenched her hands together trying to stop her injured one from bleeding out. As she stumbles back to the wall she sees the four empty picture frames on the other side "Oh my, is that Biff's face that just faded onto the frame. Oh no now there are three more empty frames. Seven frames, one has Biff's face, six more, Oh on, no, no, no!" she runs down the hallway yelling,

"Becky! Becky! Biff! Dale where are you guys! We got to get out of here!!!"

Becky's Room

She's still in her world of ecstasy as she continues to dance with Ray, as he, or it continues to lick all around her neck. As she falls deeper, deeper under it's spell, her mind begins to wonder *"Mmmm this feels so good. Why can't it be like this with Biff? Ah yes, I love feeling his tongue on my face and neck. And his hands, mmmm his hands are all over my body, my breast, my ass, my shoulders, my?"* she pauses for a moment, she asks as her eyes open, "Ray, why do I feel more than one pair of hands touching me. She turns her head and sees it "What the hell are you?! You're not Ray!" she yells,

It answers **"No, I am not your Ray. But you are my Sweet Tender."**

She tries to break free, but the creature's many hands are holding her in place. The creature's teeth start to pierce through it's gums to reveal themselves so long, and sharp.

Becky screams "No!, Please no!, Please don't, please let me go. No, no, no!!!"

The beast bites down on her ripping out parts of her shoulder, neck, and face. her blood sprays from her body as she starts to feel cold. Blood spills from her mouth as she gazes into the monster's eyes, tears fall from her eyes as she cries out,

"Cough, cough. "I'm sorry, I'm so sorry."

The monster strikes again, Becky screams as loud as she could, The last sound coming from the room... **"Sweet Tender."**

Dale's Room

He's still on the bed making out with Samantha, and although he appears to be enjoying himself, his mind seem to be somewhere else, he thinks to himself,

"Wow this girl can kiss. Tiffany a good kisser too. But Samantha is so hot. Tiffany's hot too. I'm about to have sex with Samantha. But I want to have sex with Tiffany. Oh shit."

TIFFANY!!" Dale pushes the Samantha thing off him as he jumps off the bed.

"What's wrong?" she asked

He answers "Uh look, uh Sam you're great and all, but uh, I'm saving myself, for Tiffany."

she replies **"Tiffany? Tiffany? Haha, she will never open herself to you. Not in a hundred years, hehe."**

"Well if I have to wait a hundred and one years, then I'll wait for a hundred and one years." Dale responds as he wipes his face, he notices

"Ah what's this green goo on my face, and mouth? Is this your saliva, ugh." He looks directly at her "What the hell are you? You're not Samantha!"

she replies **"Forget, Tiffany, forget Samantha, come back to bed Sweet Tender!"** her tongue raises out of her mouth, as her long pointed teeth grow larger, her eyes turn a reddish-greenish color, and her nails elongates, in a beastly voice she says,

"Come on Dale, don't you what to suck more face? Kiss, kiss, kiss." the beast reaches for him

"Gross he yells!!" as he grabs the lamp on the nightstand and smashes it across her head, knocking her onto the floor. Dale runs out the door and tries to keep her in by holding it closed as she bangs on it trying to get out.

"Let me out Sweet Tender, let me out. I want to suck more face, Kiss, Kiss." she says as she continues hitting on the door.

Dale reacts "No, no, there won't be no more sucky-face with you, ugh!" He yells out, "BIFF! Becky!! TIFFANY!!!"

Tiffany is still running down the hallway clenching her hands together. She continues calling for the others "Dale! Becky! Biff!

Becky!!" she stops running "Becky!, Becky!!, Becky!!!" Tiffany hears a voice from behind, "I'm here Tiff." she turns around "Becky, I'm so glad to see you." Tiffany tries to hug Becky but was unable to as she passed right thought Becky.

"What the hell Beck? What happened to you" Becky answers, "I'm dead Tiff."

Tiffany replies "What? No, no it can't be. what happened Becky, you're a ghost?"

Becky answers "This is all that is left of me, a beast looking like Ray. It ate, it ate me."

Tiffany replies "It can't be," Another voice speaks "It true Tiff, we're both dead."

Tiffany turns and sees "Biff! Not you too!" she starts to cry,

Biff tells her "Don't cry for us Tiff, it's too late. There's nothing here, but death. Run Tiff run leave before it gets you."

She responds "But I can't just leave you guys here. And where's Dale?"

Biff answers "Dale is fighting for his life right now. Go to him, and both of you get out of here, before we're all lost."

Becky says "Run Tiff, go. Go now. Get to the road by 6 O'clock and you will be save."

With tears in her eyes Tiffany begins to back away from them to make her escape saying her last words to them, "I Love you guys."

They both smiles at Tiffany as she turns and runs off.

Biff takes Becky by the hands and says "I'm so sorry, about the way I treated you, Beck."

Becky smiles as a ghostly tear run down her face,

Just then a beastly voice shouts out as something attacks them **"You belong to us Now!!!,,, Yum!"**

Tiffany could hear their ghostly screams which burns to her soul. Tiffany finally sees Dale, she asks "What the hell you're doing!"

He answers "I'm trying to keep the monster in the room, so I can stay off it's menu." "Uh a little help?"

Tiffany lean against the door to aid him, she asks "Uh. Why you without a shirt?"

He replies "It's a long story. Where's the others?"

"They're dead!" she answered.

"What!!" he yelled.

Once again she answers, "They're dead, and we got to get back to the road by 6."

Dale looks down at his watch and Yells, "Dammit, it's almost 6!"

73

<u>Meanwhile Back on the road</u>

"There it goes again." said Pookie.

"Will you stop it!" Donna yells.

Ray adds, "Yeah man, just because all the houses look the same, doesn't mean it's the same one."

Pookie leans back into his seat saying "Oh, it's the same house. We've been driving in an endless loop ever since we passed through that beam of light earlier."

Donna responds "You're crazy, and I've had just about enough of you Pookie."

Ray yells "Enough both of you!"

Pookie calmly says "You been driving for hours Ray, but you'll see when we pass it again."

Donna says "Dam you Pookie, dam you."

NIGHT ON THE HAUNTED HIGHWAY

Back at the House

Dale and Tiffany are continuing to hold the door keeping the beast inside, Tiffany says "We got to hurry before more of those things come!"

Dale reacts "There's more!!"

Just then the banging and the shaking of the door stops. They both ease away from it, Dale grabs Tiffany's hand and says as they start to run,

"Come on baby, we got to get the hell out of here!"

A few moments later they reached the front door, they stop to catch their breath.

Dale says "Come on we're almost there." Just as they start opening the door they hear a loud crash from behind.

"What the hell was that?" Dale yelled as they both turned around to see.

"Oh my lord. What is that" Tiffany yells, as they both stood bewildered by the giant creature that rammed through the walls. Ten feet tall, with over sized teeth, claws, large horns, and tusk all over it's body.

It rises to stand on its back legs, while its front arms pound its chest, it's lets out a monstrous roar.

Dale sees a broom and grabs it yelling to Tiffany "Go, Tiff, run while I'll hold it off."

She answers "What?! No I'm not leaving you!!"

He replies "Better one of us make it out of here, then none of us." he pushes her to the door then yells, "Go now Tiff, run!"

Dale stands firm to face the beast, as Tiffany runs out the door, jumps off the pouch, catches her balance, and continues running.

Just then the beast crushes through the front of the house as Dale's body is tossed from its hand. The monster lands then raised pounding it's chest, roars, and starts to chase after Tiffany.

Ray, Donna, and Pookie are about to pass by the house, Pookie raise up "Hey isn't that Tiffany coming form the house?"

Donna answers "Yeah, it's Tiffany. Why is she here? Why is she running?"

Pookie answers "You don't see what's chasing her?"

Ray stops the car and yells, "What's the hell is that."

Donna Yells, "Tiffany!!" as she tries to get out of the car,

Ray grabs her arms yelling at her, "Are you crazy that thing will get you too. Stay in the car!"

Pookie yells, just stay in the car!" as he jumps out.

Ray asks "What are you doing Pook?!" "I'm gonna help Tiff get in the car, once we're in, Ray you hit the gas!"

Ray agrees, "Got you Pook!"

Donna yells out the window "Run! Tiffany run as fast as you can!!"

Pookie also yells, "Come on Tiffany, you can make it, come on girl!!"

Dale's body lands a few feet in front of Tiffany, as she runs past his broken body she tries not to look, but she can't help it.

Crying she can now see Donna and Pookie cheering her on to run faster.

She hears a voice, "Tiff." she answers "Dale, that's you?"

He replies "It's me baby. Remember how I taught you to run faster, sprints Tiff, on your toes, head up, focus on Pookie focus on... No, no get away from meeee!"

a monstrous voice says to Dale **"You belong to us!!"**

Tiffany starts to cries as she hears Dale scream, she can feel the beast closing in on her, she lifts her head, and begins to run on her toes, as she completely focuses in on Pookie.

"That's it girl you got this!!" Pookie yells

She can now feel momentum pushing her faster as she jumps into Pookie's arms. Using her momentum he turns as he grabs her which launches both of them into back seat of the car.

As the beast leaps toward them Pookie yells, "Go, Ray! Go!"

Ray slams on the gas and the car speeds off as the beast just miss them. It recovers itself pounds it's chest, and roars louder than before. it watches them drive away.

Ray yells, "What was that thing!!"

"It's alright Tiff, I got you, shhh. You're safe now, you're safe." Pookie said as he tries to comfort her.

"Tiffany, What is going on?!" Donna asked.

Tiffany answers, "They're dead. They're all dead."

Ray yells, "What?!"

Donna asks, "Who's dead Tiff? Who?"

She answers, "Becky, Biff, Dale. They're all dead." tears flows from Donna's eyes.

Ray displays anger pounding on the steering wheel "Dammit!, Dammit!!, Dammit!!!" he shouts.

Pookie says "I told you. Didn't I tell you? I been saying all night. But did you guys listen to me? Noooo!"

Ray explodes, "Shut up Pookie! Just shut your dam mouth once and for all!"

Donna says "Ray calm down."

Ray explodes again, "I'm sick of him!" Pookie responds "Fuck you Ray. You should've listened to me in the first."

An awkward silence filled the car for a moment.

Donna turns to Tiffany grabs her hand, saying, "Well Tiff, at least it's over."

Tiffany raised her head and ask, "What time is it?" Donna looked puzzled as Tiffany repeats "What time is it?!"

All eyes looks at the clock on the car's dashboard. After a few seconds of eerie silence.

The time is 5:58 am

Ray says "Fuck!" Pookie looks up and yells, "Look out! Ray look out!!!"

Ray looks up from the clock, he sees the beast he thought they left miles back running towards them hard, and fast "No freaking way!!!" he yells as the beast launches itself in the air, Ray tries to hit the breaks, but it was too late as they meet head-on.

CRASH!!!

.They all scream, as the Beast roars, and then darkness. A scary voice saying **Sweet Tenders.**

8:19 am

The first Responders are on the screen, doing what they do, picking up the pieces, cleaning up the place. Sheriff Buckley is in the thick of the miss as he holds a conversion on the emergency phone box on the road,

"Yeah, yeah, we counted seven. Eh, the four white kids we meet at Stinky, and the three black kids, that stopped for gas late last night. No, we only found four bodies, but we think all seven of them are dead. I know, but what can we do? We tried to talk them into staying over, but those kids wouldn't hear it. What else could we do? Hell we build a whole party zone to keep the kids off this road at night.

What? No, no last I heard Samantha's still alive, guess she didn't say too much as Frankie Lee did."

One of the paramedics waves at Buckley, he responds "Hold on Mayor."

He asks, "What is it Stew, I'm a little busy!"

Stew answers "Sorry Sheriff, but we got a live one here!" Buckley answers "What? well you know what to do!"

He returns to his conversion with the mayor, "Well, mayor it appears we've got a survivor. Yeah, yeah, I'll meet you at the hospital. bye." he hangs up. He thinks out loud *"Dammed kids."*

He yells out "Alright people, get this mess cleaned up before the traffic picks up!" he leans in close to one of his deputies saying, "Roy I'm headed to the hospital with the survivor, I'll catch you back at the station later. I'm leaving you in charge here."

Roy replies "Don't worry boss I'm on it,"

As Roy walks off barking orders to the others. Buckley shakes his head saying, "Dammed Kids." He gets in his squad car and, leaves.

END

<u>Epilogue</u>
<u>*One of the many secret bases in*</u>
<u>*America's military*</u>

Major Hank Hawkins is walking through the hallways at a steady pace. He arrives at his destination, knocks on the door, he hears a voice saying "Come in." he enters, salutes, and reports,

"General Albright. Sir it happened again. The Goodwind Phenomenon."

Albright responses "Thank you Major. I'll take it from here. Dismiss." Hawkins replies "Yes sir." He salutes, and leaves.

Albright grabs the phone, dials, he speaks "Colonel Whitmore, it's Albright. Mobilize agents Beauty, and Beast. I got a mission for them." he hangs up thinking, "Now finally, we're gonna get some answers, and put a stop to this once and for all."

<u>Cast:</u>

"Biff"..Bernard Becker
"Dale"..Donald Dole
"Ray-Ray"..Raymond Pierce
"Beck"...Becky Bradshaw
"Tiff"..Tiffany Thomas
"Donna"...Deanna Dean
"Pookie"..Percival Pierce
Mr. Frost..Teacher
Buckley...Sheriff
Stinky/Stinkmeijer ....Bar and Grill Owner
Davy Lockheart....................................Old Guy 1
Jake...Old Guy 2
Samantha..Waitress/Store Clerk
Bartender...Himself
Stacy Sullivan......................................Bodybuilder
Mark Maryland.....................................Quarterback
Mary Maryland.....................................Classmate
The Old Lady..?
Clifford..Butler?
Mee,..?
Myy,...?
Bee..?
Dee..?
Not Ray..?
Little girl..?
Not Samantha.......................................?
The Beast..?
Stew..Paramedic
Roy..Deputy
Frankie Lee..The Sheriff's Friend
Ms. Molly...Preschool Teacher
Linda Lawson.......................................Cheerleader
Missy Monday......................................Cheerleader
Connie Kane...Mother
Cornwallis "Corny" Kane.....................Son
Cassie Kane..Daughter
M J...Store Clerk

<u>Mid-Credit</u>
<u>*Back at the Quick-E Q Mart*</u>

M J is pricing and restocking the store, just then he hears the front door bell "Ring Dinggle-Ling." Two men enters.

M J thinks to himself, *"Hump, two middle-aged gentlemen, wearing suits, ties, dress shoes, and shades. They must be Feds."*

They look around a bit, one ask the other, "Have you ever seen such a quaint little shop like this before?"

The other answers, "Yeah, in a slasher movie."

They both chuckled a bit, then stopped as MJ walks toward them.

He asks, "May I help you gentlemen?" The first one says, "My name is Curt Stoner. This is my twin brother Case."

Case pulls down his shades, and nods his head as a greeting. MJ, returns the greeting, then says,

"Yeah well, that's all good. Is there something you fellows are looking for?"

Curt responds, "Yeah Mark Jeremiah Jericho. Your country needs you."

Mark Jericho drops his head, shaking it as he yells out, "OH HELL NO!!!"

Welcome to New Breed Publishing Home of Paperbacks, Comics, Mags, Audio, and E-Books packed full of Action, Adventure, Fantasy, and Horror. Great Stories, Heroes, and Monsters are all here for your Entertainment and Escapism. Welcome to the fun, the excitement, the mysteries, the all-out chaos, and the greatest adventures. Welcome to the New Breed.

NIGHT ON THE HAUNTED HIGHWAY

Be Sure To Checkout Some of Our Other Books.
<u>Out Now</u>

Darkness looms in the city that never sleeps which threatens the lives of its citizens, and the only ones who can stop it don't even know what they are truly dealing with. But with the aid of a mystery man, New York's Finest is ready to serve and protect the people. The only questions are "Can they?" and "Just how far they're willing to go?" For When Evil Walks, Death Follows.

Amazon, Barnes & Noble, Apple iTunes, Google Play

<u>**Coming Soon**</u>
Code: Name Axel

Raised, and trained by one of the world's most notorious assassin clans, sold off to be an agent, and secret weapon for the US. She's out to prove that she's the most lethal killer on this Rock. Not only must she take out America's enemies, she must also battle with demons of her own. Demons who are detained to break her... we'll see.

Late Summer 2023

Shadow
Chronicles of Evil

Jack the Evil caused much havoc, death, and dismay in the Big Apple. But how in the world did such evil come to be? What was the driving force that would set such a beast against Man and his Woman, and how can Man defeat such evil? To defeat Evil one must understand it, to understand it one must trace it back to its roots, and see how it all began. So before Evil walked, it had a Chronicle.

Fall 2023

<u>Post Credit</u>
<u>*6 pm. Hallway 166*</u>

This piece of road stretches between
the towns of Goodwind, and Bryce City. Both townships and their residents understand that nighttime is not the right time to be here, so unless there are outsiders, no movement will be happening here during the witching hours. But tonight there appears to be an explosion of activity, for there is something afoot. Movement coming from the house that seems to only appear at this late hour. Someone or something has come out of it, its headed towards the road. It appears to be somewhat human, but who can say for sure.

As it walks toward Goodwind a dark, sinister voice echoes in the gloom.

"One has survived. Go soldier do as you must, do as you will, whatever it takes. Let nothing stand in your way...

...And bring back "The One That Got Away."

The Soldier fades into the night.